Unhallowed Murder

A Murder-Mystery Romance

Candace Blevins

KALEIDOWORDS Publishing

Candace loves hearing from readers! You can find her online at:

- Website – candaceblevins.com
- Facebook – facebook.com/candacesblevins
- Facebook group – Candace's Kinksters – facebook.com/groups/CandacesKinksters/
- Twitter – twitter.com/CandaceBlevins
- Goodreads – goodreads.com/author/show/4489132.Candace_Blevins

Stay up to date on Candace's newest releases
and get exclusive excerpts by joining her mailing list at
bit.ly/cb-new-release!

It's Halloween night and the Haunted Corn Maze is a madhouse. However, no one knows one of the zombies in the diorama is a dead body. There's a reason it looks so real.

Lieutenant Veronica Woods is dressed as a Power Ranger, as are her four friends, enjoying the frights and scares in the chill autumn air. Ronnie is a tiger-shifter, and her sense of smell points her to the body, but there's no logical reason for her to climb the small hill and traipse through the display. At least, not until she scents a group of vampires, and she bullies and coerces one of them into helping her report the crime so she can begin her investigation.

Josef is an ancient vampire with a military mindset. He was a general in his human life, and now he's head of security for one of the most powerful vampires alive. He hasn't had a personal relationship in decades, and has no interest in one, but the adorable little tiger shifter walks like a sex kitten and issues orders like a military general. Her people obviously respect her, and he finds he doesn't want to leave her side when she's ready to turn him loose.

Chapter One

Josef looked in the mirror and shook his head. How had he let Kendra and Fawne talk him into this? Dress slacks, no shirt, and these insane plastic fangs. Was this *really* how society expected a modern day vampire to dress? At least the historical vampires were clothed respectably.

He heard the laughter of old friends on his way down the staircase and smiled despite himself. Abbott with Spence, Kendra with Eric, and he and Fawne weren't an item, but it was nice neither would feel like a fifth wheel. He loved seeing the light in Kendra's eyes once again — Eric had given her a reason to find joy in life, and while Abbott hadn't needed a reason, he, too, was much happier now with Spence by his side.

Josef didn't need a partner to give him purpose. His job was to keep his coterie, his family, safe. He was head of security, and while the buck might stop with Abbott, Josef ran their security team of werewolves and tech geeks. The tech geeks were a new addition, but Josef had learned to roll with society's changes over the millennia.

He hugged Kendra, Fawne, and Spencer, shook Eric's hand, and gave Abbott a small bow — enough to show respect without being over the top. Josef grew up in the military and appreciated knowing the chain of command. Such things were important.

Abbott and Spencer were dressed as vampires from the twelfth century, with Abbott as high royalty, and Spencer as a young man. Their scent clearly told him Spencer likely wore a plug and some kind of chastity device so the young wolf couldn't touch himself or get hard.

Kendra and Eric were dressed as if from the fourteenth century — Kendra as a queen and Eric as her loyal knight. Josef was aware the two often switched up their power exchange relationship, which meant Kendra would likely be in charge when they enjoyed themselves in private later.

Fawne's outrageous ball gown made her look like a Disney princess, complete with tiny waist and too-perfect hair. She'd gone so far as to add extra red on her lips, dripping down as if she were a messy eater. Delicate little Fawne *never* made a mess with her meals.

And Josef had at least managed to be a modern day vampire. They'd wanted him to dress in a roman general's attire, which was fitting, but he had no desire to go back to that time. The shoes are *so* much more comfortable in this century.

"Are we ready, then?" Abbott asked, his hand on Spence's back.

"We can all fit in my Q7," said Josef. "We should take it instead of the limo, so we don't draw so much attention." At Abbott's nod, Josef stepped back to allow Abbott and Spence to exit the room first.

As with all holidays, Halloween had drastically changed over the centuries. Josef tended to be cynical about these made-up social constructs, but he'd agreed to take his shirt off and spend the evening with the other leaders of his coterie. His family.

They started at a Haunted Hill not too far from the coterie house, and then drove north of the city to a Haunted Corn Maze. They'd do Dread Hollow later, and the haunted show inside the Ruby Falls caverns last.

Josef smelled the dead body on the walk from parking lot to maze, but wasn't overly concerned. From the smell, the person had died the night before, but he didn't recognize the human's scent so it wasn't his concern. They were there to have fun.

Candace Blevins

Chapter Two

Ronnie stood in front of the mirror, hands on her hips, and blew out a breath. "I can't believe I let ya'll talk me into this."

"At least you have the figure to pull it off," said Mandy. "I'm over here showing every damned curve I have."

Ronnie turned and pulled her friend into a hug. "You're beautiful just as you are, and don't let anyone make you believe otherwise."

The five women had been close friends since high school, and while some of them had drifted away right after getting married, or while their kids were babies, *everyone* had been able to make it tonight. Amy had made their Power Ranger costumes from unitards, which — as Mandy had said — hid *nothing*.

Only two of the five didn't have children, and Ronnie was happy to be an honorary aunt to their kids, but had no desire to become a mom. Her career was her life, and if her friends didn't practically demand she spend time with them, it might've become *all* of her life.

Getting ready together was part of the fun of these nights, and Amy's kids were with her ex-husband, so they were using her house for the pre-party. The women talked about kids, boyfriends, husbands, sex toys, and a book about to come out from their favorite author. Ronnie was happy she'd come, and she relaxed into the energy of the group. It was nice to step away from talk of homicide. The dead would be waiting for her tomorrow.

But she'd made enemies in her line of work, and that meant she rarely went anywhere unarmed. No one said a word when she looped her cross-body mini-purse over her shoulder and situated the bag at her hip. At least she'd brought her deep blue one that closely matched the blue Power Ranger color.

The evening was cool, but Ronnie was fine in the long-sleeved unitard. Her human friends brought jackets in case they needed them, but didn't intend to wear them.

The Haunted Corn Maze was a madhouse of kids and adults, with most everyone in costume. Ronnie immediately identified it as a security nightmare, but tried to ignore those thoughts so she could have fun. The cop in her was *always* watching though, as was her inner tiger.

They rode the haunted hay ride first, and screamed when the guy ran after them with the chainsaw — which she assumed didn't have a chain on it. They ducked when the giant spider dove at their heads and barely missed, and just all around had fun reacting to everything the ride tossed at them.

The group stopped by the restroom when they got off the hayride, and made their way to the refreshment area. Ronnie's cheeks tingled from the chilly night air, and hot chocolate would hit the spot. Mandy bought a funnel cake and insisted they all help eat it — and Ronnie happily took her up on the offer and then bought another to share. Shapeshifters need a lot more calories than humans, and her friends were always jealous that she could eat whatever she wanted and stay skinny. In truth, the tiger wasn't a fan of the sugary snack, but she wasn't going to buy a burger right then.

Amy looked longingly at the plate, and Ronnie pushed it closer to her friend. "We're going to need our strength to walk through the haunted maze — you can afford a few calories!"

"I got hot cider instead of hot chocolate." Amy scrunched her nose. "I don't think they'll go together."

She probably had a point. "Do ya'll want to walk through the arts-and-crafts section? Or go straight to the maze?"

"Let's do that last, in case we want to buy something," said Amy. "I'm hoping the woman with those beautiful quilts is back, but no way do I want to carry a heavy blanket through the maze."

Fifteen minutes later, they rounded the huge barn to head to the maze, and Ronnie caught a hint of something.

Something dead.

The closer they got to the maze's entrance, the stronger the scent. She doubted any human smelled it, but it was impossible for her to ignore.

They neared a zombie diorama set up on a hillside, and Ronnie zeroed in on the smell. One of the fake zombies was a dead woman, but she couldn't go traipsing past the phony crime scene tape to investigate without a good reason. She turned and scanned the crowd, took a deep breath... and smelled vampires.

Chapter Three

Josef heard the voice before he zeroed in on the young female tiger broadcasting so loudly.

I need assistance. Please let me know you hear me. I need assistance. Please let me know you hear me.

It came over and over, as if a mantra, and it was a tiny bit louder with every iteration.

Answer her. She's police. Abbott's voice came into his head, over the tiger. His Master believed one can never make too many friends in high places.

I hear you, tigress. What do you need? He could see her thoughts — he knew what she needed, but there was no need in making her uncomfortable. She'd be happier if she had to tell him.

She breathed in relief. *I'm with the Sheriff's Office, here with human friends. There's a dead body, but there's no way I can point it out. Do you think you can make an employee notice the extra zombie and investigate, and then scream and carry on when he or she discovers it?*

Josef scanned brains until he found someone who'd fit the bill. A young woman returning from the bathroom and headed back to the maze. He put the suggestion into her head to notice it hadn't been there before, and then to duck under the crime scene tape to check it out.

I have done so. She's returning from the restroom. Give her a few minutes.

Can you look in her memories? Was the victim there last night?

She was not in the display last night. I checked her memory of how it looked when she arrived today at four, and your victim was there. They opened at noon. Let me find someone who arrived then.

It didn't take long for Josef to find the man in charge of security. He'd noted the victim was an addition, but had assumed someone had decided the display needed more. He hadn't checked — but he was human and had no reason to.

Your victim was in the diorama at noon when they opened.

Ronnie slowed and turned to watch an employee climb the hill, her eyes sharp. As soon as the young woman screamed in horror, the Lieutenant stepped into action, showing her badge and identifying herself as a lieutenant. The property's security personnel followed her orders without question, and when uniformed deputies arrived, they did as well.

Everyone did as she said. Without hesitation. The young tiger female might be small, and dressed in a ludicrous blue skintight costume, but she exuded authority, power, and control.

"I'm going to stay with her and see if I can be of further assistance," Josef told the rest of his group. "I'll arrange for a car to be brought so I can leave when I wish. Enjoy your evening."

Abbott accepted the keys when offered, and he gave Josef a curious look, which Josef ignored. He'd gotten involved and he wasn't ready to walk away yet. Or, that's what he kept telling himself. He was certain it had nothing to do with the way he could see the Lieutenant's muscles flexing and moving under the costume she wore, much as a tiger's muscles — nor with her confident command of so many people. *No.* He'd gotten involved and now he was part of it. He wasn't ready to leave yet.

He texted one of the coterie's wolves with orders to bring his F-PACE, a charcoal dress shirt for him, and size three women's jeans along with a suitable lightweight pullover shirt. Abbott kept a closet full of new clothes in a variety of sizes because, *well*, because they were a house full of vampires, and their guests often discovered the clothing they arrived in wasn't fit for them to leave in. Josef wanted his F-PACE because it seemed fitting to drive a tiger around in a Jaguar, but he didn't think she'd be impressed with a sports car. She was far too practical.

The sexy, competent Lieutenant noticed him standing in the shadows, but didn't say anything. He'd *suggested* to everyone else that he belonged, but as of yet, hadn't put any suggestions into her head.

Right off the bat, the Lieutenant ordered crime scene people, extra lights, a better photographer, and arranged for the employees to be taken to the barn while guests were asked to leave. She requested more uniformed officers as well, to help get everyone off the property safely. A Detective Carter arrived — a large, imposing, heavily muscled African-American man — and the two worked seamlessly together.

A quick dip into Carter's head told Josef the detective respected his Lieutenant and her expertise immensely — and her authority, so long as she didn't needlessly put herself in danger. The male detective was human and didn't know the Lieutenant Detective was a tiger, so he didn't understand some of her decisions.

Lieutenant Woods handed jobs out, gave orders, and had the crime scene efficiently organized soon after taking it over. Twice, she made a call to someone with a higher rank to apprise them of the situation, but not to ask what to do — merely to let them know what was happening, and that they needed to get the PR team engaged because she was certain social media would be buzzing.

Josef never allowed himself to get involved with someone younger than five hundred years old, and had kept to his rule for well over a millennia.

But this young woman fascinated him.

Her friends had known that once someone had found the body, they'd lost her for the night. She didn't even apologize, just told them to be safe and assured them she'd find another ride back to her car.

Josef intended to be that ride.

He listened to her thoughts, and discovered they were as disciplined as the rest of her. She had a map in her head of what needed to be done and who she trusted to handle each item. When the medical examiner finally arrived, Josef noted this man was the first to comment on her Halloween costume.

"The Blue Power Ranger? Really? I'd expect you to be in nothing less than Red."

The Lieutenant chuckled. "My friends doled out colors based on skin tone and what looked good on us, not on personality." She looked to the dead body. "I'm guessing the gunshot to the forehead killed her, but I'm not qualified to say that officially."

"Got it in one, Lieutenant. The darkness around her eyes appears to be makeup, like maybe she had makeup on and someone tried to wipe it, but made a mess. Same with the redness around her mouth. The bruising around the wrists is real — I'll verify later, but it looks as if someone zip-tied them. Probably goes without saying, but she wasn't killed here."

"No. Did she start in the dress, or did they put her in it? It fits in well enough with the zombie motif. Maybe she was already wearing it, and they ripped it in a few places? It's a casual fall outfit, not terribly dressy, especially with the cardigan over it." The Lieutenant looked at the dead woman's feet. "One shoe. We'll need to look for the other.

A nice, sensible shoe, dressed for comfort and looks." She sighed. "The hair mussed and draped over part of her face hides the bullet hole. Can you give me time of death yet?"

He shook his head. "She's been dead more than... twelve hours. Possibly eighteen. I assume you want me on this right away and it can't wait until morning?"

"I'm sorry. You're in a costume, too, but this is already all over social media, and our bosses would like this closed fast, if we can."

Paying visitors were still being shepherded out, but most were in their cars, snarled in traffic. The only people close to the crime scene were police personnel — the employees were still sequestered in the barn. Still, a telephoto lens from the parking area would be able to get a nice shot, and she'd reminded her people of this several times.

Josef, of course, still watched from fifteen feet away, standing in the shadows. None of her people seemed to notice him, so she let him stay. Josef couldn't pick up on her reasoning, but didn't dig to find out.

While her thoughts stilled and she took in the scene once again, he addressed her telepathically.

I realize one of your people offered to take you back to the station, but I can give you a ride. You have your own lie detector skills, but I can offer to let you know what people are thinking when you question them, if you'll let me ride along. As you can tell by your people's reaction to me here, I can easily make them accept my presence.

What will I owe you?

I make no demands or requests.

I can't have you beside me when I interview people. You can make the people present accept your presence, but not the people who might see you in pictures or video later. If you can remain in the background and help, I'll accept your offer. Tell me your name, please?

I am Josef.

Well, Josef, I'm going to interview the security guards and the people who were here during the day today, preparing for the big night. I'm hoping we'll have an ID on her by the time we finish, in which case I'll go to her home and see what I can learn about her from her things.

She turned to Detective Carter. "Josef will drive me when I'm ready to leave. Please look the scene over once the body is removed to be sure we have all the evidence we need. I know the crime scene techs did, but…" She sighed, and refrained from pointing out they'd missed bits and pieces in the past. "If we get an ID, I'll let you know so you can meet me at the victim's house."

"You shouldn't go alone, Ma'am."

"I'll stay outside and wait for backup if I sense anything amiss."

With Josef letting her know what each employee knew as they were brought to her, she spent a minimal amount of time interviewing the staff before dismissing them and thanking them for their cooperation. No one knew who the victim was. All were horrified a dead body had been so close and they hadn't known. The fact it was Halloween seemed to make it even more perverse to them.

She talked to the manager last, and asked him about any no-show employees. She received two names, got their addresses, and nodded to Josef as she walked out.

As soon as they were both in the vehicle and the doors were closed, she told him, "Thank you for your help. I don't understand why you've stayed, but I appreciate the offer to continue helping."

"Your people respect you."

"Goes both ways. What do I need to know about you? I'd like to know more than a first name."

"I am head of security for The Abbott. Did you recognize him in our group?"

"I did not. I know my own leader as well as the Amakhosi, and I've had occasion to deal with the Wolf Alpha. I've also been made aware of the leadership of the RTMC, but only because of my job. That's the extent of my knowledge of the supernatural power structure."

"Most people do not get along with Martin."

Her thoughts agreed with him, but she said, "Martin has his own reasons for the way he chooses to lead."

Josef's respect for her went even higher, though he hadn't thought it possible. She didn't like the tiger alpha either, but she wouldn't speak ill of him. This woman had more valor and honor than any of the recently-born he'd met this century.

"You're going to question the two men who didn't make it to work?" He knew she was, but he wanted an excuse to hear her voice.

"Someone knew when they'd be able to get the body into the diorama without being seen. My people are still going over video, but I don't expect them to see much from it, either."

Her phone rang, and she answered with, "What do you have, Corey?"

Josef could easily hear both sides of the conversation.

"We got a hit on her fingerprints, since she works for the post office. Her name's Wendy Abrams. Bad news — the FBI flagged the case as theirs."

"Send me her address anyway, as well as the name and number of the FBI agent on the flag, please." Within moments, she had him on the phone. "Agent Graham, this is Lieutenant Woods, HCSO. How is it you think Wendy Abrams' murder is a federal case?"

"I was already working a crime involving the victim, regarding her employment through the postal service. Her death doesn't end my obligation to solve her case."

Josef observed her thoughts as Lieutenant Veronica Woods analyzed the FBI agent's voice and attitude, and then formed a strategy — all in a split second. "There are things the Feds can do better than the local Sheriff's Office, but I can do other tasks better than you. My guess is that when I find the murderer, it'll solve your crime. I'd like to suggest we work together. I can search her home while you question her supervisor and coworkers, and then we'll meet, compare notes, and figure out whether we can continue to move forward together." She took a breath.

"Assuming of course, there's a record of your conversations with them."

A twenty second pause, where the Lieutenant assumed he was looking her up, and she felt confident he'd agree to her proposal once he saw her solve rates.

"I believe we can make that work, Lieutenant. Full disclosure on both sides."

"And if our superiors order us not to disclose something, we'll let the other know we're being constrained by using the word pineapple in a sentence."

He sighed. "Agreed. You've worked with us before?"

"Something like that. Is eight a.m. okay for a meeting? My murder room or yours?"

"I'll bring my people to you. There'll be three of us. Make it eight thirty."

"I look forward to meeting you in person, Agent Graham. In the meantime, can you give me the short version of why you were investigating Miss Abrams?"

"She'd informed her superiors of an attempt to bribe her, and we were looking into it. She didn't have much information about the male who called her. He'd used a burner phone, but since he knew her personal cell number, the assumption was that the suspect either knew her or someone close to her."

She thanked him again and disconnected.

"I don't suppose you can tell if someone's lying over the phone?"

Josef hedged. His Master preferred not to let other shapeshifters know the limitations of his top people's powers. "Sometimes. I wasn't trying with your FBI agent, but since I haven't met him and I don't know where he is, it would've been iffy."

Chapter Four

The vampire had given a mostly non-answer, which was what she'd expected.

Ronnie took a moment to call another of her detectives and instruct him to question the two employees who hadn't reported to work. When she disconnected, she asked the vampire, "How far into my head are you?"

"I have given you no suggestions, and I don't intend to do so."

"You didn't answer the question."

"I can easily monitor your thoughts. I have not attempted to delve into your memories, and at this time I have no intention of doing so."

"There's a reason the rest of us don't like being around ya'll."

He chuckled. "Since I see your thoughts, it's only fair I tell you mine. However, you need to focus on your case right now. Let me know when you have time, and I'll share them."

"Out with it, while you're interested in sharing." Most vampires preferred secrecy.

"I was a general when I was a human, many, many centuries ago. I respect the hierarchy, and I place importance upon traits like honor and valor. I see all of this in you, and you've earned my respect. I will assist you with this case, and when it's over, I hope you'll consider spending time with me in whatever way makes you comfortable. I would very much like to get to know you better."

Martin would have a cow. Or, on second thought, he might order her to have a relationship with Josef, to curry favor with the powerful Strigorii coterie. "Is there a need for me to tell you my reaction to that?"

"Logical, with more practicality than humans are usually capable of under the circumstances."

Ronnie's thoughts flashed to the time Martin had ordered her to be food for a vampire, and she quickly pushed the thought away and focused on her case. Josef didn't need to know the confusion she still had around the experience. She'd intended to hate every second of it, but it had been oddly fulfilling.

"If she knew her killer, she may have let him into her home. On the other hand, if she'd been told she likely knew the person who bribed her, she may've been cautious about

inviting people in who hadn't been in her life in a while."
She sighed. "Why leave her at the Haunted Maze? *Dammit*,
we need to find the crime scene." With any luck, she'd been
killed at home, but Ronnie didn't expect to get lucky.

"The killer likely has her phone and purse. Or, had it.
Once Corey has her phone number, he's going to find out
it went off the network sometime last night, and for now,
we'll assume that's the likely approximate time of death."
She glanced at the vampire beside her. "Thank you for
having whoever brought you a shirt, also bring me jeans
and a shirt." She'd already thanked him, but felt she needed
to again. Before he could respond, she asked, "What
country were you a general for?"

"Rome."

"Anyone I'd recognize?"

"Without looking through your memories, I have no
way of knowing how much you know of Ancient Rome."

"My father was a history professor. My bedtime stories
were full of war and blood."

"You understand, I'm over two thousand years old and
I've lived under at least seventy different names since then,
yes? Different lives, different professions, different
nationalities, different personas. I'm no longer the man who
led both army and navy."

They were approaching the victim's home, and she
told him, "Drive by slowly, so I can get a layout of the land.
Make a circuit around the block and come back, please. I'm
hoping I can see a little of the back of the house from
another road."

She was silent as he drove by. No signs of a person or people, and no car in the driveway.

"So you aren't going to tell me who you were? What happened to leveling the playing field?"

He sighed. "You don't pull punches. I like that about you. I was once Gnaeus Pompeius."

"Pompey the Great? Really?" He made the turn onto the road behind her victim's house, and peered between the houses in the hopes of getting a view of the back of Wendy Abrams' home.

"We'll pick this conversation up later. You need to focus on your victim."

"No lights on in the front or back of the house. She lived alone so I don't need a warrant. Her vehicle isn't in the driveway, which might mean she wasn't killed at home, or it could mean they used her car to transport her body, to avoid DNA evidence in their own vehicle."

He turned back onto the victim's street, and she said, "Turn your lights off now, please, and come to a slow stop in front of her house."

She had good eyesight even when human, but she let her tiger rise enough so she could look out of the cat's eyes.

"Standard doorknob, no deadbolt. I should be able to get in without calling a locksmith." Because the county preferred the locksmith fee over having to pay someone to install a new doorframe and door. "Would you do me a favor and hang out in the backyard, just to be sure no one exits as I'm entering?"

Josef was silent a few seconds. "There are no active brains in the home — sleeping or awake."

Ronnie smiled at him, despite her misgivings. "You're kind of handy to have around. Okay, I need you to stay out of the house, because there are going to be crime scene techs all over the place at some point, and you don't want people looking at your DNA." She pulled a ponytail holder from her small purse and put her hair into a bun at the crown of her head. Next came some gloves and her lock picking tools.

"I assume you can warn me telepathically if anyone approaches?"

"I can, Lieutenant."

"My friends call me Ronnie."

"You'll let me know when it's okay for me to use your familiar name, then."

She looked straight at him and thought, *You big dufus — I was telling you it's okay.*

He chuckled. "Touché."

It took her less than twenty seconds to get in the front door. She turned the living room lights on and verbally announced her presence to the empty house because it was protocol, and it felt wrong not to. Silly, since no one was there, but whatever.

The house looked to have been built in the sixties, with a fireplace someone had probably called art deco back then. The kitchen was a combination of old and new appliances — a diarrhea green stove and a black refrigerator. There was no dishwasher. Horror of horrors.

The living room and kitchen were one room, and a hallway led to three bedrooms and a small bathroom. One of the bedrooms had been turned into a workout room, one was a guest bedroom, and the other was the master bedroom, which boasted another bathroom.

Nothing seemed out of place — no reason to think there'd been a struggle, but the scents told another tale. Terror. Anger. Rage. She breathed and memorized the males' scents. Two of them. One was likely her boyfriend, but the other had abducted her, and she'd been terrified.

However, there was no blood and no smell of bleach. They'd abducted her from her bed and transported her elsewhere to execute her. Had they entered with lock picks, jumped her while she slept, zip-tied her wrists, and forced her to walk to her own vehicle to be driven to her execution?

No. This was a nice neighborhood — the kind where neighbors call 911 when they hear screams. However, with the large yards and buffer of trees between houses, neighbors might not have heard her scream from inside the old brick house.

Had they crammed something in her mouth to keep her silent? Or would the medical examiner discover duct tape adhesive on her lips?

There was no doubt this was one of at least two crime scenes, but she couldn't order the crime scene techs based on scents only a supernatural could smell. She stood and looked at the room, trying to find a reason to call for them.

The bed was unmade, but most people didn't make their beds, so unless family members insisted otherwise, this likely wasn't unusual.

There wasn't a bedside lamp. Had it been broken in the struggle? A cord was plugged into her alarm clock, and her phone had likely been charging on her nightstand when they took her. Ronnie pulled her phone from her pocket and texted the FBI agent.

> *When and where did her cellphone fall off the network?*

Agent Graham had been in contact with the victim in recent days. He'd have that number and had no doubt already checked.

> *Her home. Shortly after two this morning. Check the microwave.*

Sealed phones don't allow you to easily remove the battery. So sometimes the bad guys dunk the phones in water to kill them, but sometimes they thought they were smart by microwaving them. Leave them in too long and you get fire, but she hadn't smelled smoke. She checked anyway, and other than noting the microwave desperately needed a good cleaning, she saw no signs it had been used to kill a cell phone.

Agent Graham's information gave her a reason to request the crime scene techs — if her phone fell off the grid here, it was likely her abductors had been here. She made the call and looked over the bedroom once again.

Josef, a deputy should be here soon. He'll camp out on the front porch and wait for the crime scene techs. I shouldn't be much longer.

You have me until about an hour before dawn, Lieutenant. Do what you need to. I'm good.

She took pictures of every room from every wall, and then walked through with video going. The uniformed deputy she'd requested was on the front porch when she exited the home, and she instructed him that no one came in or out until another detective showed up with the crime scene unit.

She made a call to Corey, her tech guy, on the walk across the yard, back to the car. "Has anyone else used the victim's home as an official residence since the she moved in?" He'd get around to checking that eventually, but she needed to know now.

"A boyfriend who seems to've moved out two years ago, but I have another lead to check out — social media has given me a first cousin with a shitload of priors."

"Nothing on the ex-boyfriend?"

"He's living in Virginia. Do you want to see if I can place him in town recently?"

"No. Tell me about the cousin."

"A long list of minor and then minor-ish offenses up until six years ago, when he was convicted of possession with intent. Spent a few years inside, moved to Chattanooga when he got out, and went off parole three months ago. Quit his mandatory day job the next day. Gang task force has some notes on him — he's CHM."

CHM was Clifton Hills Mafia, one of the local Latino gangs. She sighed. "Address?"

He hesitated a few extra seconds before giving it to her, and she thanked her lucky stars she had such a great team. She'd been in situations where she hadn't been taken seriously as a woman cop, or had been hated for having a higher rank than the men under her, but her team respected her while trying to make sure she stayed safe — they never crossed the line of being insubordinate while trying to protect her, but they stepped right up to it on occasion. It was both frustrating and heartwarming, because they wouldn't try to stop her if they didn't care, but she could take care of herself.

While she typed the address into Google maps, she told him, "I only plan to drive by and scout the area. I won't take action without backup, Corey."

Corey was the only member of their team who wasn't a sworn officer, but he was worth ten times his weight in gold.

"He has ties to the local cartel connection, which is probably why Agent Graham was brought in on the original case."

"What do you know about this agent?"

"Specializes in gang activity. Our notes say he's in tight with the RTMC. He's the agent who was instrumental in bringing down Thomas Pickering."

Pickering had been a corrupt District Attorney, and the Chattanooga PD was still trying to recover from the cluster-fuck. Graham had stuck up for the MC because it was important they be brought down the right way, and crooked cops pissed him off. She instantly felt better about her little deal with the agent. "Thanks."

Her victim had been late twenties and Caucasian, but the cousin was listed as Hispanic, and he lived in the Clifton Hills area — ground zero for the new *brown* gangs springing up and battling for power.

She detested the black/white/brown terms, but it was hard to insist on different terminology when the gangs in questions used those terms to describe themselves.

Josef drove them to the cousin's house and made a slow circuit without needing to be told. Of course, he could hear her thoughts, so she shouldn't be too impressed.

Kevin Ramirez lived in a rundown duplex, the yard desperately in need of a lawnmower. "There's a nightclub about a half mile away. Any chance you can read the brains in this house from there?"

"No one's home. The occupant of the other half of the duplex is in the same gang, but doesn't appear to know anything about your victim."

"Well, damn. Thanks for trying."

"Certainly. Can I ask you to text me from your phone, so I'll have your number, please?"

"I'm not…" She sighed. "I don't think I can give what you asked for, earlier. The idea you know everything in my head is just… *creepy*."

He started to protest, and she added, "I know you said you're only hearing my thoughts and not diving into my memories, but it's... I'm sorry. I just can't."

"I will answer the questions your father had about Sulla."

"How did you—" She cut herself off mid-sentence. He knew about her father's questions because he'd been in her head. *What else had he seen about her father?* She quickly cut that line of thinking off and focused on the list of things she needed to do. "You aren't helping your case."

"I didn't dig for anything. I only saw what you recalled to memory. I will always be honest, unless Abbott or the Concilio orders me not to be, and in that case, I'm not opposed to agreeing to the same deal you requested of the FBI agent — a safeword, so you'll know I've been given orders I don't agree with but must obey."

"And if we actually need to speak of pineapples?" It wasn't likely to come up in the course of an investigation, but who knew what conversations she might have with an ancient vampire.

He chuckled. "We'll need a different word. Onomatopoeia, perhaps?"

A smile blossomed on her face before she realized she was going to. "Yeah, that works."

In the end, she texted him, but only because he offered to help her when she interrogated suspects.

Josef could tell the little tiger shifter female was directing her thoughts away from several areas of thought. He picked up whispers of attraction, glimpses of her controlling her reactions by focusing on her case instead of what she really wanted to think about. She'd liked him without a shirt, and had been disappointed when he'd put one on, but then had convinced herself it was better that way, so she wouldn't have to police herself to keep from staring at his chest, and at the area near the top of his pants. He wondered if she'd even realized the thoughts were there, at first. Eventually, she'd aimed her thoughts firmly at the case, and redirected them if they came off it for any reason. The human had incredible discipline. He knew centuries-old vampires who couldn't direct their thoughts so well.

He didn't want to lose contact, so he stayed in her head once he dropped her off at her friend's house, where her car was parked. He tailed her from three quarters of a mile behind her while she drove — close enough to monitor her thoughts, but not close enough she'd see him following her.

And he couldn't resist the smug smile on his face when she finally thought she could think freely. She wondered what his bite would be like, and her entire body went fevered just thinking of it. Martin had ordered her to feed another vampire once, and she'd intended to hate it, but she'd liked it so much, it'd scared her.

Her thoughts were a jumble — this was the woman considering and *feeling*, and no longer the purely logical detective.

The bottom line? She was attracted to him and had managed to keep those thoughts from her mind while he was with her. She didn't call to mind lessons of someone teaching her the process of redirecting her thoughts — had she figured it out on her own?

He hadn't given her any suggestions because his little tiger shifter was so strong willed, he had a feeling she'd recognize the suggestion. This was exceedingly rare for humans, but since shapeshifters knew to be on the lookout for it, about fifteen to twenty percent sometimes realized.

And he'd instinctively known not to try it with Lieutenant Veronica Woods.

So much power and control in such a beautiful package.

He could've gone farther into her mind while she slept, and he was tempted. However, he wanted to know about her childhood, about her first sexual experience, about her siblings, and more about those friends she'd arrived with. They'd talked her into wearing a skin-tight costume, and he had a feeling she'd only do that for really good friends.

But he didn't explore her memories because he wanted to learn about her a little at a time. He wanted her to share herself, and that wouldn't happen if he spent the night going through her head while she slept.

Chapter Five

Ronnie was in her office handling the details of another murder when the FBI team entered. She finished up with the detectives, made sure they were clear on their goals, and stepped into her murder room.

"Agent Graham?"

The attractive agent tilted his head, introduced the men with him, and handed her a file. "This should catch you up on the details, but I can brief your people of the highlights, if your team has time?"

"We do. Let's move into the conference room, the rest of my team is already there."

She was in charge of the Violent Crimes unit, which consisted of a dozen deputies and detectives, plus three civilians. Most seasoned detectives were partnered with either a deputy or a junior detective, but she handled the toughest cases herself, and her personal quick-response team was made up of five people, including Corey the tech geek. When the brass wanted something solved right-the-fuck now, her team jumped into action.

Agent Graham noted the pearl paint on the back wall, and set a small projector on the table. The Feds always had the cool tech. He used his phone to move through his presentation while he talked.

"Wendy Abrams was a twenty-seven year old postal carrier. Her mother's younger sister gave birth to Kevin Ramirez within a few days of Wendy's birth. The two children played together and were close until the sixth grade, when Kevin's parents moved to Nashville. Kevin joined a Latino gang there, had some run-ins with the law while a juvenile, and finally went to jail for a few years as an adult. He came to Chattanooga to live with his uncle when he got out of prison. Six months later, he rented an apartment, which he moved out of when he came off parole. The duplex likely offered less prying eyes to his illicit activities once he was engaged in them full time, but an important note is that several gang members live in the vicinity."

"The CHM doesn't let gang members fully step back into their roles until they're off parole," said Detective Jamison Carter. "Smart, really, and I'm glad the other gangs aren't in the same habit."

Agent Graham nodded agreement and continued. "The Inspector General's office asked us to take point on Miss Abrams' case because the FBI is better qualified to handle cases involving gangs and the cartel. There was no wrongdoing on the part of an employee, and no mail was actually sent, which limited their scope and allowed them to farm it out to us."

Ronnie hated that the beginning of every briefing had to include why each department was given the case, but she'd learned to let the FBI guys talk while they were in the mood, because all too often getting information from them was worse than pulling teeth.

"Miss Abrams was approached via her personal cellphone in an attempt to bribe her." Graham switched to a graphic showing arrows moving from the southern coast of the U.S. to midsized cities all over the country. "The Cortez Cartel has started using the post office to distribute their product. The largest cities have sophisticated sniffing equipment, but the mid-sized cities have cheaper, slower versions, so only mail fitting a certain profile is sent through it. The bad guys know this, so they ship their goods from, for instance, Naples, Florida to Chattanooga, Tennessee, coming from a homeowner in good standing and shipping to a homeowner in good standing, and nothing is checked because it bypasses every system that might flag it as suspicious. The trick is in sending it from and to the right people."

Another man stepped forward. "They bribe a mail carrier on both ends. For today's discussion, we only need to tell you they ship it to an upstanding citizen, and they pay the mail carrier to hand the package off to them instead of delivering it to the proper address — the going rate is five hundred dollars cash, and once the pattern is established, they often send a package a week."

Another agent continued the explanation. "The handoff usually takes place in a parking lot without security cameras. Several local gangs work for the Cortez Cartel, and the Clifton Hills Mafia, usually called the CHM, has been gaining ground. Your suspect was high ranking in an affiliated Nashville gang before he was convicted of dealing. He started near the top locally once he was off parole."

Agent Graham changed slides and continued. "Ramirez isn't in charge yet, but I feel it's only a matter of time — assuming Flores, the current leader, doesn't kill him to keep him from taking over. But, back to the bribe: It's likely they had another gang member make the call, since the victim would've recognized her cousin's voice. She reported the caller having a Spanish accent, so from there it isn't far to suspecting her cousin and his associates."

"It didn't occur to you that she might need protecting?" This from Deputy Myers, who had a protective streak eons deep.

"Our threat analysis didn't put her in danger," said Agent Graham. "I asked her if she felt as if she might be in danger for filing the report, and she said she did not." He flipped to the next slide and looked to her. "Here's my list of what happens next. Do you have anything to add before we figure out who's doing what?"

Four items on his list were checked off: the APB on her car, obtaining a list of known associates, getting a search order for the cellphone records of the cousin, and interviewing her immediate supervisor.

"You can check off searching her home. I typed my notes up already, and we should get the preliminary report from our crime scene people soon." Her eyes scanned the slide again. "Not on the list, but completed — we've interviewed two people who didn't show up for work at the corn maze. No reason to suspect either, but you'll have the information anyway."

Still to do were interviewing coworkers, notifying the victim's mother, talking to the medical examiner, and a whole host of smaller items.

"I planned to ask Corey — my tech guy — to find a connection between a known gang member and the Haunted Maze. Whoever killed our victim knew about that diorama. Staging her as they did possibly means they wanted people to know what happens if you turn down an offer from their gang. Why else do something so public? They're banking on the fact we'll release details of the case, which will give them street cred. I vote that — when it's time — we merely report her cousin joined the gang and she got caught up in the mess through no fault of her own."

Corey flipped a tablet on and looked up. "Auto theft finally got the location of her car from the manufacturer. Strip mall parking lot about ten miles from the maze. Crime scene tech's heading that way with a rollback."

"Assuming they killed her somewhere else," Ronnie mused, "drove her to the maze in her own car to keep from getting her blood in theirs, and then parked it — how did the bastard get home?"

"I'll check cabs, Uber, and the like," said Corey.

"Do it because we have to follow every lead, but he didn't use them. Can we find out where the car travelled that night?"

"The manufacturer claims they don't log that information. They can search for a car and find it, but they don't keep track of where every car is."

"And he killed her phone at her house. He's smart. I hate when the bad guys are smart." She glanced at the large black man sitting to her left a second before meeting Graham's gaze again. "Detective Carter helps our gang task force when they need more bodies. He tells me Kevin Ramirez shot straight to the top of the hierarchy when he arrived, due to his rep in Nashville and then in Pikeville. We should aim him at the gang related tasks." Pikeville was the Tennessee state prison where Ramirez had resided.

"We'll need known associates while he was in Pikeville, too. We need to know who he made friends with inside." This from Sergeant Detective Perry, her stereotypical grumpy old detective who took in everything and missed *nothing*.

"I can handle that, too," said Corey. "I have a murder board started." He flicked his tablet and the interactive whiteboard lit up on the other wall. The room was silent while everyone took in the pictures of the victim and her cousin, pictures of her house and the outside of his duplex, various crime scene photos, and a note of everything missing — like the victim's car, purse, and phone — and everything they needed to further investigate. Cory took the FIND sticker off the stock picture of the victim's car. They'd replace it with a picture of her actual car soon.

"This is good," said Agent Graham. "I have no problem working from your software, since all of you are used to it." He met my gaze. "I propose we let your team mainly focus on the murder, while my team focuses on the gang and cartel angle. While they do that, you and I should notify the mother and then the cousin."

Ronnie's Captain had told her Agent Graham was straightforward and good to work with as long as you were upfront with him and you were competent. She was pleased with him so far, but she'd been burned by the Feds before. However, his proposal made sense, so she nodded and added, "Once we talk to Ramirez, we'll need to put someone on him. Might not be able to keep him alive, but we should show the effort." Protection was just an excuse to tail him and monitor him, but it cut through a lot of red tape.

Agent Graham grinned. "Excellent plan."

Between the two of them, they handed out all tasks to their people with no disagreements. When they finished, she motioned for her team to get to it, and everyone left except Deputy Myers, who'd be coming with her.

Agent Graham eyed the large former-marine a few moments before saying, "I assumed you'd ride with me."

"That's fine. If there's room for Deputy Myers, I believe you'll find him an asset. If not, he can follow us."

"There's room."

"Good. We can discuss our game plan on the way."

Notifying family came with the job, and it never got easier. Wendy Abram's mother had completely fallen apart. Ronnie's heart broke for the woman, but she had to put up a wall to shield her own emotions or she'd never be able to do her job. She breathed energy in, remembered the pain and vowed to bring Mrs. Abram's daughter's killer to justice, and then stepped away from it emotionally.

The notification was behind them, and she had to leave it back there.

Agent Graham drove them south of the city, towards Ramirez' duplex. Wendy's cousin lived barely a mile from Georgia, but thankfully he was still in Tennessee and in Hamilton County, where Ronnie had jurisdiction.

Ronnie was itching to do more than talk, but she breathed in patience and calm, and read through the reports out loud as her team posted them.

"Bullet to the head was a nine mil. Confirmation of zip-ties on her wrists. Cotton threads in her mouth mean something was likely stuffed in it to keep her quiet. It also appears the bastard raped her both vaginally and anally. Doc will check medical records to see if there's a notation about being allergic to latex, because there's some kind of chemical burn at both locations. He figures it's from a condom because smart rapists are careful about DNA these days."

She paused on the term *smart rapists*. It pissed her off, but she needed to focus. She turned in her seat and met Myer's gaze. "We have the list of known associates while he was inside. Can you pull it up and see if you recognize anyone?"

He'd been texting someone, and he looked up. "Corey sent me the list when he got it. One jumped out at me. Corey's getting an address now. Asshole's still on parole, so we can search without a warrant." He shrugged. "CHM doesn't usually let their people in on anything profitable until they're off parole, so I doubt we'll find anything. Might not be worth tipping our hand."

Kevin Ramirez once again wasn't home, and she wondered if he'd skipped town. He hadn't been home at midnight, and now he wasn't home at nine thirty in the morning.

Ronnie called Corey, who answered, "LT."

"I want to talk to the uncle that Ramirez moved in with when he got out. Where does he work?"

She heard Corey's fingers clacking his keyboard. "He works for a roofing company. I'll call and find out where they have him today."

"Please tell them he isn't in trouble, but we need to talk to him about a family member."

Candace Blevins

Chapter Six

Josef awakened in his bedroom at the coterie house and looked at the clock. Nearly four thirty. He reached out with his mind but couldn't find the mouthwatering Lieutenant Veronica Woods. *Ronnie*.

He'd asked Abbott to send breakfast, and he reached out with his mind once again to see who was in the house. *Ahhh*. His Master had sent him the spicy little smart-assed journalism student. The little wolf was currently in their living room, doing homework on her laptop.

He telepathed her image to one of the werewolf security team. *Bring her to me.*

One of the nice things about dying instead of sleeping was that he could get ready for the next day before dawn took him. He opened his door to let his breakfast in, and motioned towards his settee.

"You're only on the menu for a feeding, but in that little miniskirt, I'm wishing I'd asked for someone fuckable."

This young lady wasn't opposed to fucking, she just wanted to be able to pick and choose, depending on her mood. Josef could clearly see she'd have taken him up on it if she didn't have plans for later. Still, it would've only taken the smallest *suggestion* to sway her, but that wasn't playing fair.

Besides, Abbott didn't allow his people to manipulate the thoughts or willpower of his sheep without express permission.

Josef didn't make her turn him down verbally. No need in making things awkward. She hadn't taken a seat yet, so he sat in his wingchair. "Sit in my lap. I can come in from behind and keep from mussing your hair. Do you want pain or pleasure? Orgasm, or not?"

"Pain, with an orgasm at the end, please." She shook her head. "What if I lean against the wall and you do me from behind? Can I use your facilities to fix my makeup?"

The image in her head had him in her ass and tears flowing down her cheeks. The little thing was *craving* pain, and she knew from experience his cock was thick.

"Of course, *deliciae*." It wasn't often he could use Latin and be understood, but Amara smiled at the term of endearment. It roughly translated to delight, or pleasure, and this little thing was certainly both.

Would the little tiger want him to feed on her alone, if she accepted him as a lover? Or would she understand a powerful vampire must feed from his full political spectrum.

Or would she even accept him as a lover?

Since he understood Amara didn't want to muss her hair, he ordered her to lift her miniskirt to her waist, remove her panties, lean over the back of his settee, and grab the wooden arms. She had to stretch to reach, but she managed.

"Give me permission to compel you to hold on."

"Permission given."

"*You will not let go until I or my Master commands it.*"

He'd removed his pants and underwear already, and he put the barest amount of lube on his cock. The girl wanted pain.

Josef could enjoy all kinds of sex, and didn't *need* to hurt his partner to reach orgasm, but he enjoyed the occasional sadistic encounter. Plus, her blood would be divine with the chemicals released during what he intended to be a brutal ass-fucking.

Candace Blevins

Chapter Seven

Josef's afternoon was taken up with duties involved in keeping Abbott's properties and people safe. He loved his job, but he wished he could check in with his little tiger. Once he'd fed from her, he'd be able to find her mind no matter where she was in the county.

He finished his most pressing tasks before sunset, and was contemplating whether to text her or merely show up, but she texted him first.

> *If you're still in the mood to be helpful, I'd love having a mindreader nearby.*

He couldn't help his grin.

You pulled me into this case, and I'd like to see it come to a satisfying conclusion. Where shall I meet you?

Are you in a place you can talk?

He pressed the button to call her, and smiled at the sound of her voice. "*Bellula.* I hope you are doing well this evening."

She hesitated a half-second. "Little beauty?"

"You know Latin?" He didn't mean to sound as surprised as he did.

"I told you my father was a History Professor. I assumed you'd learned more."

"And I told *you* — I only observed your memories as you recalled them. I didn't dig for more."

"Yes, you did. Thank you for that. My suspect is in a nightclub your boss owns, which means you're technically head of security there, too. Yes?"

"Which establishment?"

She told him, and he leaned forward. "He owns it through a series of corporations. How did you connect him with this club?"

"Nathan helped me negotiate for a list of clubs owned by The Abbott a while back, and I receive updates when he buys or sells. It's helpful for me to know these things."

Yes, he imagined it was. If there'd been negotiations, she'd be restricted from using the information in official channels. However, knowing ahead of time where she was likely to run into supernatural politics would be a big help.

Josef relaxed back into the chair. He needed to figure out how close his little tiger was to the Amakhosi. She lived on the east side of the county, not far from the Amakhosi's Pride. The Lion King likely allowed her to *change* and spend time on his land, which probably didn't sit well with the local Tiger Alpha.

Also, he'd need to talk to his boss about letting him know when someone received this kind of list. It had likely been done back when Abbott and Nathan were on good terms, so it'd been a friendly conversation, and not official.

"I can be there in thirty minutes. I'll stay in the back room, out of sight," he told Ronnie. "Should I need to come out, do you want your coworkers to think us strangers, or shall we be acquainted?"

"You were around me last night too much for me to try to pass you off as a stranger. I know you put out a vibe so they wouldn't notice you, but a lot of pictures and video were taken."

"I put my body into a frequency that doesn't show up on photo or video. I'll either not be in the photos at all, or will appear so blurry no one can make out my features."

"Let's tentatively plan for you to stay out of sight. If that won't work, I'll *think* at you to let you know how to proceed."

Josef's chuckle made her nipples harden from across the phone connection. Nathan had told her it wasn't likely Josef could read her mind from halfway across the county, so she should be safe thinking what she wanted while talking to him on the phone, but she didn't know how she'd manage to control her response to him when they were in the same room.

It couldn't be helped, though. They were storming the nightclub in ninety minutes, and she wanted Josef there if she could get his help without owing him anything.

A judge had granted a warrant for them to monitor two cellphones — Kevin Ramirez, the victim's cousin, and Jorge Flores aka Calacas, because he was a known close associate and his girlfriend worked at the Haunted Maze.

Flores had told Ramirez to meet him at the club at nine, and Ronnie would be there with Detective Jamison Carter on a pretend date. Carter was black, so the two of them wouldn't seem out of place. Probably. Their intel said black and brown both frequented the place, with the occasional white girlfriend. Josef verified their intel but said she'd have to dress the part.

Ronnie broke down the basic plan to Josef, and ended with, "Flores' street name is Calacas, which is the decorative skull or skeleton you see on—"

"Day of the Dead. I'm not involved with this location enough to recognize a particular patron, but I'll check with the people who are."

"He has tattoos of a bunch of Calacas on his arms, if that helps. I feel guilty about asking you to be there when I'm not going to acknowledge you. I don't know for sure when I'll get away from work tonight, but I'll text you when I do, so we can meet somewhere."

"Not a problem. I'll go to the downtown Billiard Room when I finish with your project. Meet me there when you can."

Chapter Eight

Ronnie had a small wardrobe unit in her office, where she kept shoes and clothing for nearly any occasion. She changed out of her pantsuit and into low, tight jeans and a skimpy spaghetti-strap shirt, with her gun in a bellyband under the jeans. It showed if you looked for it, but no one would stop her in that part of town. She slid a second magazine and some zip-ties into the slots of her belly band, and refastened her jeans.

Her hair fell out of her bun and cascaded around her face, and she added a thick layer of eyeliner and red lipstick. Finally, she sat and chose a temporary tattoo — she'd bought a variety of the heavy-duty realistic kind a while back, and should probably reorder, but the Cheshire cat would be perfect for the evening. She put it on the front of her shoulder, so the tail wrapped down and around her arm. She cut off part of a geometric design and put it on her inside right wrist.

No one ever scoped her and Jamison as cops when they went in undercover. Granted, they were usually only under a few hours, and never more than a few days, but still — they could pull it off.

She strapped her boots on and walked to the mirror on the inside of the wardrobe's door. A few adjustments to her belly band, some bangles on her wrist, her badge in one pocket, phone in another, and she was good to go.

Jamison had gone home to get his motorcycle, but he was already back when she walked into her murder room.

He'd put on athletic shoes so white they hurt her eyes, jeans, and a snug t-shirt that showed every damned muscle.

It was really too bad she didn't date humans. She also didn't date anyone she worked with, so he had two strikes against him, but he was a good friend and a great partner.

Her men whistled and sent catcalls floating around the room, and she rolled her eyes at them and walked out. Carter would follow.

Agent Graham waited for them in the parking lot, and he handed them both an earpiece. The FBI utilizes tiny little one-use dots you stick to the skin just inside your ear canal. With her long hair, the county's earpieces were fine for Ronnie, but Jamison's hair wasn't even a quarter of an inch long.

This wasn't the first time Ronnie had ridden on Carter's bike, so it didn't seem odd to wrap her arms around his oh-so-muscular torso and lean into him. She wanted to enjoy the ride, but there was too much to think about and consider, and they were there before she knew it.

Ordering food and drinks in a bar was always tricky, because they couldn't drink on duty — especially right before a situation where they might need to discharge a weapon — but you can't go into a bar and order a Coke without arousing suspicion. She could drink several beers and have zero percent blood alcohol thirty minutes later because of her shapeshifter metabolism, but she couldn't explain that to Carter. Or to her bosses.

However, this bar served beer in the bottle, which meant they could pretend to drink and no one should notice.

Josef's voice came into her head. *I'll make sure no one notices.*

Thank you.

God, she was going to have the voice in her head, the voices in her ear, and people talking to her in real life. She was used to dealing with two conversation, but three was going to push it.

I'll keep that in mind.

No — tell me what I need to know. I'll sort through it all. Don't hold back to try to make it easier on me.

Carter leaned in and put his mouth to her ear. "Waitress at three o'clock, that table is known CHM. Booth in the back corner is a bookie and his muscle."

Ronnie wondered why the Master Vampire owned this not-so-fine establishment, but didn't ask Josef.

"Two workin' girls at the bar," she told Carter, her mouth to his ear. "I want cheese fries and Buffalo wings."

The bar in the center is lined with bulletproof material so we can attempt to keep our employees safe. The Abbott owns establishments that cater to all walks of life.

He needs to put his hand in all *the cookie jars?*

Josef's telepathic chuckle was as sexy as his real one. Not that this one wasn't real, but… she shook her head and focused.

Carter ran a proprietary finger over her Cheshire cat. "I like this. Ready for a kiss?"

"Lay one on me."

Whoever finally ends up with Jamison Carter is going to be a lucky, lucky girl. His lips landed on Ronnie's, his arms leaned her back and held her in place, and she melted in his arms. Mostly, it was for show, but this was an excuse to get into it, and she tried to ignore the vampire in her head so she could enjoy her few moments of stolen pleasure. Kissing like this was safe because it wasn't going to go any further.

The waitress had just brought their food when Sergeant Perry's gruff voice vibrated through her ear piece. "Flores. Entering the parking lot in an older model red Toyota Supra. He has two men with him. Neither are Ramirez."

Ronnie stole one of Carter's fried mushrooms and then hand fed him a bite of her Buffalo wing. She made him pose for a couple of silly selfies, cajoling him like a girlfriend might, and the dude on the other side of the bar finally stopped watching them like a hawk.

Most people look at Detective Jamison Carter and a see large black man with a shaved head and enough muscles to have played college football, and they're right, but they miss the part where he got a psychology degree with a minor in criminal justice while football paid for his college education.

Ronnie's hackles went up when Flores walked by and she picked up his scent. He'd been in Wendy's bedroom. She couldn't tell her team, but she *knew*.

Flores stopped three tables away from them, across from a man who'd been sitting alone. Flores gave a brief nod of respect, said, "Tigre," and waited for the older man to motion for him to sit before he made a move. A show of respect and deference.

Ronnie bumped Carter with her shoulder while they ate, a signal that she could hear Flores and Tigre's conversation. The men knew she could hear things they couldn't, though they didn't know just how much she could hear.

"Fuckin' smurfs are looking for Spyder," Flores told Tigre. "He stayin' with some cunt in the Knob. Gonna git himself dead."

"We need him, Calacas. You can't kill him."

Flores looked across the room like a petulant toddler who'd just been told it was bedtime and was scheming his way out of it. Some of these men were nothing but overgrown babies, throwing tantrums with guns when they didn't get their way.

"You *sure* he won't turn on us? He brought family in who ratted — he got no call to threaten me for taking care of *his* fuckup!"

65

"I'll handle him, but you were supposed to take care of her. Raping her was uncalled for and you know it."

"She had to be taught a lesson. You'd rather I killed the cunt?"

Tigre's eyes flashed. "You didn't?"

"No, esé! I fucked her to warn her she need to keep her cunt mouth shut!"

The older man shook his head, as if he didn't understand the younger generation. "Then who the fuck killed her?"

"I bent her over her goddamned bed, fucked both her holes, and warned there'd be fuckloads of mothahfuckers workin' them holes if she gabbed to the smurfs again."

Ronnie's blood pressure went through the roof, and she let the cat inside her calm her nerves. Most people had to contain their animals, while Ronnie's tiger counselled her to be patient. Cats are predators, and they excel at waiting until just the right moment to make their move.

She put her mouth near Carter's shoulder to be sure no one read her lips, and softly asked, "Do we know who he's talking to? No one's mentioned Tigre, but it sounds like he's higher up than Flores. I thought Flores was in charge?"

Jamison kissed the top of her head and moved his lips closer to her ear. "I don't remember Tigre's legal name. He keeps a low profile, but it's rumored he's the leader behind the scenes. We haven't been able to substantiate that, as far as I know, and Flores always seemed to be in charge."

Ronnie turned and inhaled, but she only picked up the scent of the wolves she'd smelled when she first walked in — the bartender and at least one bouncer.

He's human, little Tigress. We employ wolves, but you're the only supernatural customer at this time.

Ronnie cataloged the arrest warrants she'd need — Tigre had called the hit, and Flores had raped her. But who the fuck had killed her?

"Ramirez is pulling into the parking lot with a woman. Not his car, possibly hers, but he's driving. Running the plates now." Ronnie wasn't surprised Sergeant Perry had commandeered the FBI's headset. He didn't trust them to keep her and Detective Carter safe.

Ramirez intends to kill Flores. Josef told her. *If not today, soon. He's going to take El Tigre's temperature — see how he feels about Wendy being raped — before he decides whether to take Flores out in the coming days, or whether to wait a few weeks. Ramirez thinks Flores raped her and then killed her.*

And he didn't?

No.

Does anyone know who killed her?

No one here seems to know.

Thanks.

Ramirez walked in with his girl, helped her onto a barstool, and told the bartender whatever she wanted went on his tab. He finally made his way to the table in the back, but only after he'd done a thorough scope of the entire room. This man was *much* more dangerous than Flores.

He also had spider webs tattooed over much of the skin they could see, which explained the street name.

Ramirez walked to the table, turned to look the room over again, and a splintering bomb went off in Ronnie's head. She slapped her hand over her ear at the same time Carter did, as well as two guys on the other side of the room. No wonder Graham hadn't argued about the local PD being the ones inside — he'd placed his people, too.

But now they had four people who'd just announced they were LEO, because Ramirez was smart enough to check to see if any were in the room.

And they were all operating without comms, because they'd ripped them from their ears.

Carter and the two FBI agents had their weapons drawn, but Ronnie walked to the table with her hands out to the side and facing forward, so they could see she wasn't going for hers.

"It's my job to find out who killed Wendy, Spyder, but it's also my job to keep you from killing whoever you suspect did it. Flores admitted to raping her and threatening her it'd be worse next time if she kept talking, but says she was alive when he left her. Who else might've wanted her dead?"

Flores drew his weapon and was in the process of directing it at Ronnie, and she took the final four steps fast, slammed his head on the table, disarmed him, rode him to the ground, and zip-tied his arms behind his back. She couldn't carry cuffs undercover in a skimpy outfit, and the rapid-fire clicks of the zip-tie sounded sweet going around his wrists.

Meanwhile, the other men moved in and secured everyone else at the table, while a dozen uniformed and plainclothes deputies streamed in to keep an eye on the rest of the room.

"Tigre," Carter said as he marched the older man out of the room. "So many rumors about you. Which are true?"

Ronnie handed Flores off to a deputy and found Graham. "I don't care if we take them to your place or mine, so long as I get first crack at Flores."

"Pretty sure you broke his nose, so you've already…"

He must've seen she wasn't in the mood for jokes, and he stopped talking and shrugged. "My case is mostly made at this point — he raped her to silence her, and they needed to silence her because they tried to bribe her. I have Flores on both. An official confession would simplify things, and that seems to be one of your many specialties. Let's step to the side and consider strategy. How can I help with your murder case?"

Ronnie looked at him, trying to figure him out, and Josef spoke in her head. *He's an honest to goodness good guy. Doesn't want anyone to get away with murder. The offer doesn't come with strings. Well, it may, but at this time, he isn't planning for it to. Shoot straight with him and he'll repay the courtesy.*

Thank you. Again.

"While everyone's here," Ronnie told Graham, "we'll argue about who gets them. Loud enough they can hear, but not enough to be obvious. I'll win. That way, while I'm interrogating them, I can pretend I'm saving them from federal charges, but they have to cooperate or that stops."

He nodded. "Tricky, but I trust you know how to pull it off and stay legal?"

"I do."

"Well then, let's play ball."

He raised his voice. "Absolutely not! Our case came first — you get them when we're done with them!"

"Hate to break it to you, but my people cuffed them. They're ours! Take a number and I'll get back to you."

She spun away from him and walked to her people. "Get them processed and ready for me. I put a uniform with Ramirez' girlfriend at the bar. I'll talk to her here, with the threat of taking her in if she doesn't share whatever she knows."

They aren't that close. She let him stay with her and use her car because he's keeping her supplied with crack. He'll show positive for a variety of drugs — he's self-medicating to keep from dealing with his grief. She only knows he has access to drugs, he shoots off way too fast in bed, and he can be scary when he doesn't get his way. Seems to be the extent of her knowledge.

Thanks. I have to go through the motions anyway, but it's good to know.

Chapter Nine

"You took the girlfriend at her word without switching directions. I've heard good things about your interview techniques, but you seemed to go easy on her."

Ronnie could see how Graham could get that impression. She needed to go over everything they knew and form a better game plan, but his question needed answering first.

"My guys call me the human lie detector. I have to be sitting right in front of someone — I can't replicate it over video, so don't bring me one and ask me to tell you if someone's lying or not, because I can't. But, when I'm face to face with someone, I know if they're lying or telling the truth. There are exceptions — when someone's convinced themselves they're telling the truth, it doesn't come off as a lie — but I'm rarely wrong when I know in my gut whether they're being honest or not."

"I used to work with someone like that. It's a handy skill."

"Even Flores' own people thought he killed her. I can't wait to ask him face to face and see if he lies or tells the truth when he says he didn't. But if he didn't, we need to figure out who had motive." Ronnie considered all the ways she could convince him to admit to the rape again. They had him talking about it on audio, but a good lawyer might be able to suppress the recording. They needed a confession *after* he'd been booked and officially Mirandized.

"I'm going to change into a suit but keep my hair down. I want Flores to see me as the bitch who broke his nose, and I look different with my hair in a bun. If I pull it into a ponytail, I want you to come storming into the room demanding you get a turn with him. I'll tell you he's my witness and the Feds will have to get in line."

"And when I leave, you're going to point out he'll be better off in the Tennessee prison system than the Federal one?"

"No, I'll talk about how convenient it'd be for him to serve his time in the county jail."

"Could work. If I take the bribery charge and you get him on rape... two crimes, two trials, but he doesn't need to know that just yet."

"I need to talk to our gang unit about Tigre. Detective Carter says a rumor's floated about him pulling the strings from behind the scenes, but no one could ever verify."

"Same here. We show Flores as the head, with notes about Tigre in the background and Ramirez rapidly climbing." He sighed. "Tigre was invited to Jiminy's Christmas party, to his big Fourth of July party, and was on the boat trip last month. We tried hard to get ears onto that boat, but couldn't."

"You need to go with me to talk to our gang unit."

"Works for me. It never hurts for us to all get in the same room and brainstorm."

Only if everyone was sharing, but so far, Graham seemed to be.

Ronnie started with Tigre, so Flores could stew alone in an interrogation room a little longer. Her cat coiled inside her, ready to spring. A human calling himself a tiger bugged both of them.

She tossed a picture on the table of Tigre and Jiminy on his dock, drinking beer and fishing. Graham was helping in ways she hadn't expected.

"You seem to be in tight with the local cartel connection."

"Jiminy? Nah. He's good people. No one gonna put the cartel in tiny little Chattanooga. Did you break my boy's nose?"

"He says he's fine. Seems to be able to breathe okay. We offered him some ice and he turned it down." Dumbass was trying to be all macho, but in this room, every word was designed to bring Lieutenant Woods' opponent to a planned outcome — a confession.

"You told Calacas to shut Wendy up?"

"Who's Wendy?"

"You knew they'd follow the breadcrumbs back to Spyder, right? You needed her to change her story." Ronnie sat back. "Or did you mean for him to silence her forever, and he decided to try it his way?"

"I had no idea what the boys were up to. Calacas asked me to help him work out a *misunderstanding* between him and Spyder. I ain't know what the boys were up to — I was just there to help them figure things out without killin' each other."

Ronnie leaned forward. "So, you're just an old man who don't play the game anymore? Offering advice when asked?"

"Yeah."

She sat back again and looked him over. He'd stayed out of prison his entire life, despite being a very bad man. They weren't going to get a confession from him, and she probably wasn't going to trick him into saying something incriminating. Still, she'd try to put him at ease and see what happened.

"You didn't have to worry about texts and email back in the day, did you? Were pay phones a dime or a quarter when you started?"

He considered the question before answering, careful he didn't say anything she could use against him or his people. "Dimes at first, then quarters. Can't even find the damned things no more."

"None of your kids went into the life, but now you have two grandsons in it. That your choice?"

"Dumb fucks. They think college is too much trouble. Too much work. My kids all went away to college, where I could be sure there wasn't a gang to join."

"And how do you feel about the kids in it now? Spyder was eleven when he joined in Nashville, and was suspected of killing at least two people before he was finally put away for possession with intent to distribute."

He shrugged. "I can't say how they run things in Nashville."

"So, you don't let eleven year olds hang out with the big boys here?"

"I told you — I'm retired. I was asked to try to keep Calacas and Spyder from killing each other. That's the only reason I was there."

His words smelled sour. Rancid. "*Ahhh*. You were doing so good, telling me the truth, and you had to go and blow it. Just a few more questions — do you know who killed Wendy Abrams?"

"I don't think it was any of the boys."

"Hmmm. Truth. Let's try another. Did you intend for Calacas to kill Wendy when you told him to shut her up?"

"I didn't tell him to do *nothing*."

"Another lie. When he entered the bar yesterday, you thought he'd raped her *and* killed her, and weren't happy he'd done both. You thought the rape was overkill. That tells me you have some humanity in you. Warped, but still."

She hadn't asked a question, and he didn't give her an answer. Ronnie asked the question. "You have no problems

75

ordering someone dead, but raping them goes too far — is that it?"

He rearranged his cuffed hands and glared at her.

"That's okay; you don't have to answer. I find your silent response enlightening." Ronnie stood. "Hang out a while longer, sir. I may have more questions for you once I've talked to the other men."

Next up was Spyder/Ramirez, because she needed to gain as much information as possible before she confronted Calacas/Flores.

"I don't know if anyone's told you, but on behalf of the Sheriff's Department, I'm sorry for your loss."

Spyder eyed the cuffs attaching his wrists to the center of the table, and looked back up to her. "Yeah. I can see that."

Ronnie reached in her pocket and pulled a cuff key out. "You're right. I have questions for you, and you'll likely be charged in the bribery scheme, but that isn't my case." She freed his hands and sat back in her chair. "You were read your rights during booking? You understand them?"

"Yes, and yes."

"You and your cousin were close as children?"

He glared at her with no intention of answer further questions.

"Here's the deal — if you want me to find out who killed Wendy, I need your help. It's a simple question: were you and your cousin close as children?"

He rubbed his wrists. Considering. Finally, he nodded. "Yeah, but then my parents moved to Nashville, and the neighborhood kids were…" He shrugged. "You either joined the gang or you were beaten up. A lot. It was a different world. I guess I grew up one way and she grew up another."

Asking an easy question first was designed to get him talking. Would he answer a more difficult one? "Tigre assumed Calacas killed her, but he says she was alive when he left her, and I believe him. Who else might've wanted Wendy dead?"

He shook his head. "Had to be Calacas. No one else even knew about her."

"Not even Tigre?"

"He knows everything, but no one else."

"Her mother says the two of you spent some time together after you moved back to town."

"My uncle on my dad's side said I could move in with him when I got out. Once I got an apartment, my PO said I'd get bonus points if I spent time with family, so I contacted Wendy and her mom, and they had me over for dinner a few times. Wendy paid me to help her paint her house, and we talked while we worked. After that, we hung out and watched Netflix some. She cooked for me — good food."

His emotions got the better of him and he looked down. Ronnie had a hard time feeling sorry for him. He might not've pulled the trigger, but she was dead because of him.

"Did she have a boyfriend?"

"Yeah. Mickey, like the mouse. He works in the passport office at the post office. They hadn't been dating long, but they've been friends a while. She met him at church."

"Okay, that's helpful, Kevin. Next, I need to know if you called her with the bribe, or if your buddy Calacas made the call."

"I ain't a rat."

"He raped Wendy in...." Ronnie flicked her tablet on and paged through the files to her notes. "I bent her over her goddamned bed, fucked both her holes, and warned there'd be fuckloads of mothahfuckers workin' them holes if she gabbed to the smurfs again."

Ramirez rubbed his wrists, remembering the cuffs. "He made the call. We were worried she'd recognize my voice." He looked down again. "I never shoulda told 'em I had a cousin who worked for the post office."

"Is there anything else you know that will help me find her murderer?"

He shook his head. "If it wasn't Calacas, I don't think it was us."

Truth. *Damn*. But, there was a boyfriend, so at least she had another string to pull.

Ronnie stepped into the viewing room and looked at Perry. "Find out where Calacas' girlfriend lives and works. Have someone pick her up in the morning, so she's waiting for me to talk to when I get here. Don't tell her anything except she's needed for questioning." She looked at Graham. "We conveniently have people here who can probably tell us who Mickey in the passport office is."

Graham nodded, and she looked at Detective Henderson. "I'll catch Mickey at work tomorrow after I talk to Flores' girlfriend, and I'd like to know everything about both of them before I talk to them."

Ronnie walked into the last interrogation room, but didn't sit. She'd put Flores in the smallest one, with the whomper-sided table and the staticky speakers.

His face was a mess. Both eyes were dark already, and the swelling was intense.

"Oh, that looks painful. I'm told you turned down medical attention and wouldn't even accept ice to put on it?"

"I'm fine, *cunt*. Ask me your questions so I can leave."

Asshole wasn't going anywhere, but telling him that would be counterproductive. She needed him to talk, and her gut told her the friendly approach was her best bet. "I think I like smurf better, but I guess I'd be Smurfette, yes?"

He glared at her, and she leaned against a wall, looking down at him, her arms crossed. Friendly face with cop body language. "The FBI is working hard to take you away from me. Bribing a federal employee with regards to their employment is a federal crime. However, murder trumps bribery, but if you can't give me anything on the murder, I'm not sure how much longer I'll be able to hold them off."

"I didn't kill her, and that's the truth."

"I believe you, but you *did* rape her, yes? I don't have results back from the lab yet, but I have a feeling your DNA is going to be all over her bedroom."

"I don't even know where the bitch lives."

"*That*, I don't believe. You think you used a condom so there won't be DNA, but there are some pubic hairs on the bed and floor, and who knows what she has under her nails."

"Check all you want. I wasn't there."

"Here's the deal, and listen closely because it won't be open long. You cop to the rape and I won't try you for the bribery charge. The feds can move you *anywhere* once they have you, but if we can keep it local, you'll either be in the county jail or Pikeville — close to home where your girlfriend and family can visit." She finally stepped forward and sat in the chair. "The Feds want you. I need something substantial on the books to hold them at bay. Rape trumps bribery. Give me *something* so I have a chance of keeping you."

She pulled a legal pad and a pen from her bag and put them on the table. "Say the word and I'll take the cuffs off so you can write your confession."

"I need a better deal."

"I don't have one for you. Give me a written confession for the rape and I won't add the bribery charges on. I might even be able to make the weapons charge go away."

Because he didn't have a carry license, and he'd pulled a weapon in the bar. If she hadn't moved so fast, it's possible someone would've shot him, and she'd *needed* to talk to him.

Corey's voice came into her earpiece. "His dad spent time in Leavenworth, LT."

80

"You want to do your time in downtown Chattanooga, or someplace like Leavenworth or Lompoc."

He sighed and she smelled resignation. She had him.

"Take the cuffs off." He stared at the table, his eyes unfocused.

"You need coffee?" she asked while she released his wrists. Her men were probably bitching about her giving him this much freedom, but she might not get the confession if she only gave him more chain. He was on the fence and she didn't want to blow it. Besides, she'd handle him if he got violent.

"How about a Mountain Dew?" he asked.

Ronnie nodded to the camera without taking her eyes off the man in front of her. She'd probably destroyed his ego, and the cat coiled inside her was wary of him, which meant she should be, too. Freeing his wrists was the right thing to do to get his written confession, but she wasn't going to let her guard down.

She sat without moving while he wrote his account — as still as a tiger waiting for prey. When he finished, Ronnie read through it, asked a few questions, and left him uncuffed while she stepped out to talk to her people. He wasn't going anywhere, and they could see into the room; if he was preparing to ambush her when she returned, they'd know.

No one was in the hallway when she stepped out, and she leaned against the wall and found her center. She could handle the emotions of solving a murder, but rape was another story. Wendy was hers, though, and she'd stick with the case until it was solved. Ronnie was alive and strong. She'd handle whatever was thrown at her. Always had, always would.

She stepped into the viewing room, and Carter told her, "Flores' girlfriend's mother sells crap at the corn maze. Leather dog leashes and shit. The girlfriend helps her man the booth."

Ronnie blew out a breath. "Do we know which nights she worked?"

"Unknown. The mom sells whips and human collars and restraints online, but just sells the dog leashes and collars at craft fairs."

"Know your audience, I guess." She considered the possibilities. "If the girlfriend knew Flores screwed Wendy, she might've killed her in a jealous rage, but a single shot to the head doesn't equal a jealous rage." She crossed her arms. Uncrossed them. "Get me a workup on the mother, too, but don't contact her. Put the three men in holding, far from each other so they can't talk. It's after midnight. I'll plan to be back by ten at the latest. Call me if you need me before then. Good work, everyone. Thanks."

The vampire would still be awake.

If Ronnie was asleep by four and woke at nine, she'd be fine.

Chapter Ten

Josef heard her in his head before he saw her.

I'm close. Are you here?

I am. Pull around back, go through the alley, and I'll instruct my security guys to let you park in the employee lot.

Thanks.

Always.

As promised, a young werewolf directed her to a parking space. "Lieutenant. Josef asked me to bring you to him. If you'll follow me, I can walk you in the back, away from the customers."

"I have her, Jeremy. Thank you."

She looked up to see Josef in a black suit with a charcoal shirt and no tie, on a small balcony. "You've had a long day, Lieutenant. We have a rooftop courtyard. Food will be brought to you up there momentarily."

"Food would be good, thank you." She'd assumed she'd be able to place an order, but she didn't mind that he'd already done so for her.

"I brought a bottle of wine that I believe will go well with your steaks."

The building was only three stories tall, but was on a hilltop above the city proper, and was one of the taller buildings on this block. Ronnie stopped short when she reached the rooftop courtyard, lit by dozens of candles and torches. A huge two-person chaise lounge was nestled between greenery, giving plenty of privacy and a view of the night sky. "Surely that isn't up here all the time?"

"Only when we wish to use it. It's taken inside otherwise, so the upholstery isn't ruined."

He motioned her to the table. "Please have a seat, a server is—" He nodded to the female server who stepped into view.

"Six steaks, medium rare. Two loaded baked potatoes, and a platter of fried mushrooms." The server settled the plates as she told what they were, and reached for the wine. "Would you like me to open and pour, Josef?"

"Please, Cindy. If you can bring a pitcher of ice water and some more sour cream, I believe we'll be good. I'll let you know telepathically if we need anything else — no need to check on us."

She gave a small bow and left.

"You heard my thoughts and knew what I wanted."

"This bothers you?"

Immensely. She met his gaze. "As soon as you ask the question, you know the answer without me verbalizing it."

"You're a good cop, and a good person, with honor and valor. You hold yourself to a standard of high morals and ethics, even more than your Sheriff's Department asks of you. I can't imagine you'd have thoughts you wouldn't want me to know."

"I have secrets. Private shit that's no one's business."

"And you're strong enough mentally to say that without thinking the actual secrets. I know vampires over a century old who can't do this. I can't help but hear your thoughts; however, I shall refrain from digging through your memories."

She ate unselfconsciously, which relieved him. So many felt guilty eating when he didn't eat, but the tiger didn't much care. Like him, she was an apex predator. Like him, she hunted humans — she put them in prison, he drank their blood. Still, they both hunted humans. Most shapeshifters didn't. Did he feel an affinity for her because of this?

No. Or at least, not entirely. He liked the entire package — woman, detective, Lieutenant, tiger. Or rather, *tigress*, he thought with a silent chuckle.

He took a sip of wine and sat back, relaxed. He enjoyed watching her eat — he could see the tiger helping to make decisions about the cut, the choice of the next bite.

"You use this location for your office?" she asked.

"There's one here I can use, when needed. My office is at our coterie house. I own a home in the same neighborhood, which allows me to keep a close eye on our people, but it gives me some privacy."

"Why do I get the feeling most people aren't privy to this information?"

"Because they aren't. I keep a room at the coterie house, and it's my official address. Only a select few know of my personal residence." He reached out, caressed her cheek. "You're tired, Ronnie. Physically *and* emotionally. You feel responsible for your victim?"

"Yes. She's mine now. It's my job to get justice for her and her loved ones."

"You have a soldier working for you. Deputy Myers?"

She nodded. "Marine. Excellent at following orders unless he thinks I'm putting myself in danger. Actually, that can be said of most of my team. They're human and don't know I'm a shapeshifter. They feel protective because I'm a woman, but they don't treat me as less than them."

"You've earned their respect." He chuckled. "Two of them had their finger on the trigger, ready to shoot your suspect. If you hadn't neutralized him, they were prepared to do so." He lifted a brow. "They're disciplined. Solid. They were worried for you, but no more than they would've been for a male officer. They trusted you to handle yourself, but had your back. It was fascinating to watch."

"I have a great team, but you didn't invite me here to talk about them. Why am I here?"

"Because you feel obligated to come since I helped you. I'm okay with this until we've spent some time together, but I hope your reason changes."

Ronnie shook her head. "That wasn't what I wanted to know, and you know it."

He smiled. "Another reason I like you. Straight to the point. I've considered this question a good bit. Not why you're here, but why I wish you to be. Why I *need* to spend time with you. I find the answer a simple one — I like you. I respect you. I've lived a long time, and I've learned matters of the heart cannot always be spoken of in terms of logic."

"Matters of the heart? Seriously?"

He shrugged. "The spark is there; it's up to us whether we nurture it or ignore it. Is it such a crazy thought?"

"Yeah. You're a vampire. You'll live until someone kills you. I'll likely die long before then. You can't go out during the day." She sighed. "You can hear my thoughts. Could direct my mind if you chose."

"You aren't a coward, but I can understand some of your fear." He settled his phone on the table, his recording app active, and hit record. "Let me help. I'm going to put a suggestion in your head that your nails are a different color. Look at them and tell me what color they are now."

"Pearl."

Josef found the place her thoughts originated. He planted a memory of her painting them red, and then *suggested* a thought of her nails being a nice deep shade of red.

"No. They aren't red, they're pearl! I felt you doing it!"

He nodded and turned the recording app off. "It seems we didn't need the recording after all. A small percentage of shifters aren't easily suggestible. This doesn't mean it's impossible, but it means any who try run the risk of being caught at it. The chance of it working is greater when you're emotionally tired, which you are now, or when the suggestion isn't far off the mark. It's possible I could've made you think white, but you rebelled at the thought of them being red."

"Also, I knew to watch for it."

"Yes, but I have a feeling you'll always know your thoughts versus the ones planted by someone else."

"So, you're saying it's hard to ignore my thoughts, and you could snoop through my memories if you chose, but you can't change my mind?"

"I can teach you to shield your mind. I'm surprised Martin or Nathan hasn't already done so. You may not be able to keep a Strigorii out, but you'll likely know when one comes in, at least."

She looked sheepish. "One of the adult female tigers was supposed to teach me as a teen. We didn't much like each other, so she just taught me enough to pass the test. I remember I'm supposed to put a wall up, but it seemed stupid, so…" She shrugged embarrassed.

"Imagine a mylar balloon big enough for you to put your whole body inside, except it isn't made of mylar, but whatever your bulletproof stuff is made of. Put yourself in it. Think about how strong it is. How nothing can get past it."

He heard her thoughts as she processed the order, and then her thoughts went quiet. He hated the distance, but she *needed* to be able to do this.

"Good job. I can't hear your thoughts anymore." Honesty was important to both of them, so he added, "No doubt, I could get around it with ease at this point, because it's new, but I won't. If you put the shield up, I'll respect your privacy. You understand I can't just *not* hear what you're thinking when your shield isn't up, right?"

She nodded. "I remember her saying that holding it is like going to the bathroom. As adults, we hold it all the time and have to make an effort to relax those muscles. As babies, we have to learn to do that. She said it's the same, and I'll eventually hold my shielding without thinking about it, but then... I never really understood what she was trying to get me to do. This seems too easy. I mean, I did it and passed Martin's test, but then forgot it."

"It's quite easy while you're thinking of it, but as you said, remembering to hold it is the trick."

She ate another couple of bites, and Josef missed the running commentary of her mind, but it was important she felt comfortable around him, so it had to be done.

"How often do you *change*? How much time do you give to your other nature?"

"It's hard sometimes, because if a high-profile crime happens, I can be called at any time, and they might understand it taking me ten minutes to get back with them if I was in the shower, but the brass expects me to answer the phone when they need me. For the longest, I'd have to take my phone with me and she couldn't get too far from it. If it went off, I'd have to *change* back to see who called."

"And now?"

"Nathan lets me prowl on his Pride's land, and I trust a few of the ladies with my phone. They have a particular song they play if I need to *change* back to human and take a phone call."

He smiled. "You don't want to tell me the song?"

She rolled her eyes. "Eye of the Tiger. It's silly, but it gets her attention."

"I look forward to seeing her. Do you let her out to play much?"

"There isn't a set schedule. Maybe two or three nights one week, all night, and then not again for a week or two. Some people drink to relieve tension, I let the cat out to play."

"How much does she help you on cases?"

"She helps keep me safe. You were in my head, so you know, right?"

"Somewhat. I could sense when you got information from her, but I couldn't sense her thoughts."

"She doesn't think in words."

"No, most animals don't, but I can usually sense their feelings, warnings, and intentions. I knew when you got information from her only because of your thoughts. She's shielding from me."

Ronnie's grin told him she liked this idea, and Josef couldn't wait to kiss those delectable lips.

Would his little tiger want to metaphorically bite back? He kind of hoped so.

"Now that you can shield your thoughts, will you tell me about who bit you, and why?"

She looked down, and he felt the distance between them increase. "Did you just wrap another balloon around the first?"

Cop eyes again. Icy cold and calculating. "Brick wall, how did you know?"

"You got farther away. Nothing more. I can't see your thoughts, I only felt the distance."

She nodded, blew out a breath, and forced herself to relax. Josef was fascinated by her control.

"Martin owed a Strigorii a meal and they wanted a female. I was his only option without having to bring someone else in. He knows better than to offer me for sex, and I guess he'd warned the vampire not to try, because he didn't do anything other than bite me physically, but…" She took a deep breath and finally looked up, her gaze one of pain and confusion. "I expected to hate it, but he made me *feel*. I didn't like it, and yet…"

Josef didn't say anything. He wanted her to finish the thought. A good thirty seconds later, she finally ended her sentence. "I'd gone to South Carolina with Martin, once the old Swan King was deposed and we were all trying to take the state back. A vampire helped us in battle, and Martin made a promise, thinking he'd offer himself. He didn't mean to offer me. He's an asshole, but he wouldn't have…" She trailed off and looked down, her shields firmly in place.

Someone had hurt his little tiger once. That much was clear, but she'd have to tell him when she was ready. He wasn't going to poke at it, and he wouldn't dig so he could see for himself.

"Okay, Ronnie. When you want to tell me more, you will. I won't look."

"Could you?"

"Most likely, but I won't try."

"I believe you. Maybe I shouldn't, but I do."

She took the last bite of the final steak, and put her fork down. "That was an exceptional dinner. Thank you."

"You're most welcome. Do you wish for dessert?"

Chapter Eleven

He'd challenged her, earlier, when he'd said she wasn't a coward. In truth, when it came to these kinds of situations, Ronnie was terrified, but was she a coward?

She liked him, and she couldn't remember the last man outside of law enforcement she'd been interested in just sitting and talking to. College, maybe? Nearly a decade ago. *Wow.*

Josef showed her whispers of something she'd thought out of her reach. He was right about the spark between them. Was she brave enough to give it energy and see what grew?

The dancing glow of the candlelight made him look dangerous — not because he was a scary vampire, but because it made him so damned attractive. She wanted those strong lips on hers, and she double-checked her thoughts to be sure they were hers. They were.

He rose, offered his hand, and the human wanted to stand without help, but the tiger put her hand in his.

Damned cat.

Music played downstairs, and Josef drew her to him in a little dance on their way to the double chaise in the shape of a wave.

Shadows played on Josef's face, letting her imagination see the vampire. Dangerous, but so damned sexy.

She'd considered calling Nathan to ask about Josef, but she wanted to do this on her own. She wanted some privacy. Tigers are lone creatures by nature, and while she enjoyed the camaraderie at work, she also valued her time alone with nothing but a good book and a nice bottle of wine.

But tonight, she was enjoying Josef's company, and she wasn't a coward.

"You're nervous and I don't know why." He spoke so softly, a human wouldn't have heard.

"Am I? Yes, I suppose I am. I don't really date. I mean, I went to high school and college, so it isn't like I'm a virgin or anything, but…" She shrugged. "I'm a little out of my element."

"And you've had a long day. As it happens, I brought massage oil up with hopes of seducing you, but I'm thinking perhaps a nice foot massage might be in order, instead. Can I convince you to remove your sexy boots, *Bellula*?"

"If I'm beauty, does that make you the beast? Or perhaps *I'm* both? Depending on whether I'm human or tiger?"

"I think the human with the broken nose would describe you as a beast." His smile told her he was joking, but he probably had a point.

"You're kind of beautiful too, you know." She felt her face go hot, and since he could no longer hear her thoughts, she felt obligated to explain. "I looked you up, saw your statues."

Josef shook his head. "In that century, a large penis was synonymous with a fool, so everyone with power had a small one on their statues." He shrugged. "There's some science behind the theory, having to do with testosterone levels and how much time you think of sex versus how much time and effort you put towards more mundane pursuits like rhetoric and complex maths, but in the end, it's more about promiscuity than penis size."

"So, you're assuring me the statue doesn't show your actual dick size? Is that it?"

He chuckled. "I suppose I am."

Ronnie sat on the edge of the chaise, hoping her feet didn't smell after being in the boots, and breathed in relief when the server brought a huge pot of steaming water, settled it near the chaise, and left.

"It's a Chinese custom," Josef said while taking his suit jacket off, "soaking the feet in hot water before a massage. I find it helps one relax and prepare for their feet to be touched."

He kneeled before her, finished unlacing her second boot, removed both socks, rolled her pant legs up, and moved the industrial sized pot so she'd be comfortable with her feet in the vessel.

"I told them one hundred and four degrees, is it to your liking?"

"It's fine. Thank you."

Josef put her totally at ease — the powerful vampire, kneeled at her feet, looking up — and then, when it was time for her to turn and lie back on the chaise, he managed to maintain the same energy, so she felt as if she were in control.

He dried her feet with a towel, lifted her, settled her back on the chaise the right direction, and finally pulled one of the dining chairs to the foot of the giant wave, so he could sit and massage her feet.

The chaise was rounded so she sat up at a gentle angle, and the second 'wave' supported her bent knees.

Five seconds into the massage, a low, involuntary groan escaped. The vampire's fingers were *magic*.

The visual of him kneeled before her had shifted when he'd moved her, so she still saw him as subservient while he massaged her feet. She was in control, still, *over* him even while he forced the muscles of her feet to relax under his oh-so-skillful fingers.

"Were you a massage therapist during one of your lives?"

"I prefer to think of them as identities, and no. I have a better understanding of the human body than most medical doctors, though." He pressed a spot that wasn't quite under her heel and wasn't quite her arch, and every muscle in her leg relaxed. Another long, low moan escaped, and Josef gave a sexy little chuckle.

Everything was fine until he started working on her toes, and heat travelled to her groin. She wondered what those fingers might feel like in other places, and suddenly, it was too much.

Josef seemed to know, and he backed off. She checked her shields — still in place. Her scent had probably given it away.

"Close your eyes for me." His tone was more request than command, so she did. "Long, slow strokes. Breathe with them. Let it happen. There you are. I'm going to match your pulse; seven beats per stroke. Find the rhythm and let it transport you, *Bellula*."

She closed her eyes and sensed him using her heartbeat as his drumbeat. It put her back in charge again. Her heart slowed, and so did his hand.

The candles flickered through her closed lids, the faint hint of jasmine in the oil soothed the cat, and the vampire's hands kept her relaxed.

The sounds of the city and traffic faded.

Candace Blevins

Chapter Twelve

Josef breathed easy when he was certain she was in a deep enough sleep he could stop. He wanted her to feel comfortable with him, and he'd succeeded. She needed to be in control, but she didn't really want to be. He'd have to help her with that, but it wasn't going to happen tonight.

He wiped his hands with a towel, took his shirt off, and settled in beside the sleeping Lieutenant. The long-lived are inherently patient, but he found himself looking forward to the day when he could hold her this relaxed while she was awake.

He telepathed for one of the wolves to come with a blanket, and he covered her while making sure the blanket stayed between them. As much as he wanted to hold her, it wouldn't do for him to make her cold. The evening was chilly, but she was a tiger and would be fine with a blanket.

Candace Blevins

Josef let her sleep several hours in his arms, and he waited until he had no choice but to wake her. He was content to merely hold her, but he had things to do before dawn, and she'd likely need to go home to get ready for her day. He'd asked Cindy to stay on duty after closing, and he telepathed down to ask her to fry a pound of bacon and a dozen eggs.

His little tigress enjoyed her food, and he enjoyed feeding her.

And so, he woke her at five in the morning with an offering of eggs, bacon, coffee, and orange juice. She was confused, then embarrassed, and then ill-tempered, but the food mollified the temper.

"You should've awakened me."

"You slept so well, my *Bellula*. How long has it been since you had someone watch over you and keep you safe while you slept?"

He heard her thoughts, clear as day. *Since before my mother was slaughtered.*

Ah, and it seemed he had some of the answer of why she felt so fiercely about the dead she was responsible for.

"I love hearing your thoughts, my fierce little tigress, and if that was intentional then thank you, but if it wasn't, I don't want to take advantage while you haven't fully awakened."

Alarm, dismay, and then distance between them once again, but that was okay. He was building trust.

"This will take some getting used to," she said, anchoring her shields and settling into them. "I appreciate the reminder."

"Thank you for not being upset with me."

She shrugged. "The tiger hunts. So does the vampire. We work around our instincts."

"You'll let me know if I can help with your investigation again."

"I will. Thank you for the offer."

"I'm going home for my repose. I'll awaken between four and five. Will you come to me when you can get away from work?"

"I don't know where the case will take me, and I don't know that I'll be able to stay awake."

She said it as a warning, but that was okay. "I'll text you the address. Bring clothes so you can sleep until morning. I'll assure you are well rested, *Bellula*."

Ronnie didn't expect to find the Amakhosi's car in her driveway when she arrived home well before six in the morning. Nor did she expect to find the King of the Lions asleep in her bed.

He didn't sit up. Just watched her from under the covers, his head on her pillow, hair mussed, eyes sharp. Stalking her. Like prey.

"Your Majesty." She didn't often use terms of respect around him, but his power saturated the room.

"Josef? What are you thinking?" He breathed in, parsing her smells. "I find that I think of you as more pride than tiger. More *mine*."

"You're saying he should request your permission to see me, Your Highness?"

So far as she knew, Nathan had fucked every adult female cat in the county except her. He'd found other ways to exert his dominance over her — he'd known it would destroy her to be forced to submit to him sexually.

He had, however, slept in her bed on occasion — usually when her life had been falling apart and she'd needed help holding everything together. In recent years, he'd done so when she wasn't home a few times, scent marking her place, probably. She hadn't asked.

"I think so. Yes." He sat, and the blanket fell to his waist. The Amakhosi was shirtless but in boxers.

Ronnie took a few steps to her left, sat on her bench, and began unlacing her boots. "He gave me a foot massage. I fell asleep."

"And he held you while you slept?"

She nodded without looking up.

"Josef doesn't date the short-lived, or even the long-lived until they're at least five hundred years old."

"He helped me with a case. He says there's a spark, and it's up to us what we do with it."

"Do you feel the spark?" He asked so softly, she was almost afraid to answer, but she couldn't lie to her liege.

"Yes, my King."

"Josef isn't going to submit to you, sweetheart."

"He kneeled before me, to wash my feet."

"Do you want me to talk to him? Explain?"

"NO!"

Nathan lifted a brow, and she corrected herself. "Please don't. I mean, do whatever you need to do so the supernatural ownership and permission thing is handled, but *please* don't tell him I'm broken."

"You aren't broken, my dear Veronica. You're one of the strongest cats I know, male or female. You just never got back on the horse. You were too young, at the time, and by the time you were old enough, it'd been too long."

She grinned. "No, I've ridden the horse, I just don't seem to be able to..." She rolled her eyes. "*Let the horse ride me* doesn't work."

He chuckled. "No, the analogy falls apart, but I take your meaning, as I'm sure you understood mine."

"I do. Thank you for watching out for me, but please let me share my secrets with him in my own time."

"Crawl into bed. You have another two hours to sleep, yes?"

"I do."

She relaxed in Nathan's arms, wondering why she didn't think of the times he'd held her since that awful night she'd watched her mother's body be torn apart.

Had some part of her brain been protecting her psyche from the vampire? Or did she merely view Nathan and Josef differently? Protective monarch versus potential lover? Could she ever have a true lover? She wasn't sure, but she was beginning to think she had to try.

"*Sleep*, Ronnie."

Nathan's voice was kind, but it was an order, and her mind obeyed.

Chapter Thirteen

Ronnie walked into her office in heels and a pantsuit, with her hair in a bun. "Is Flores' girlfriend ready for me?"

"She's all yours," Myers said. "Been stewing in the box about twenty minutes."

"Any problems bringing her in?"

"No. She's pissed, but you said not to cuff her unless we had to for safety reasons, so we didn't."

"You have a printout of her boyfriend's confession for me?"

Corey looked up from his monitor. "On your desk, along with everything else you asked for, plus the initial report on her SUV. He killed her in the back. Put the seat down, stretched her out."

So she had part of the crime scene, they just didn't know where he'd parked it to kill her. She'd have to look through the report later — she didn't want the girlfriend waiting too much longer. Corey had put the confession printout into a plastic protector, and then sealed the protector inside a heavy-duty resealable zippered storage bag. Through the layers of plastic, it looked like the original.

She walked into the room with a large purse, kept on hand specifically as a prop. Ronnie found it made her entrance feel more casual, like a girlfriend coming into the restaurant and taking her seat.

"Mariah? I'm sorry we had to bring you in like this, but I need your help. I'm Veronica Woods, and I need to ask you some questions about your boyfriend. Do you call him Jorge or Calacas?" Ronnie had verified with Ramirez that Flores' first name was pronounced *hor-hey*, and not *George*.

"He's my Jorge — my *everything* — and I ain't talkin' to no smurfs."

"So, the two of you have a monogamous relationship? Or is it okay for you to get some strange on the side?"

"*Strange*? Damn, how old are you, anyway?"

Ronnie laughed. "But it's okay, right? You can fuck who you want, when you want?"

"No, and I'd stick a bitch if I found out she fucked my Jorge."

Ah. Progress, except this likely meant she hadn't killed Wendy. It's possible Mariah just wasn't very bright, but most people don't go around making those kinds of statements if they've just shot someone in the head.

Ronnie didn't scent a lie, but Mariah's emotions were all over the place, so she needed to keep going. Not that this next piece of news would calm her down.

"I believe you, which is why I have to wonder… well, I'll just let you read it for yourself. I assume you recognize Jorge's handwriting? Or is it all texts these days, and no writing?"

Mariah took five minutes to read through it, and Ronnie was certain she read the first half and then started over again. At Ronnie's prodding, the asshole had detailed how he'd raped Wendy vaginally and anally, and had used a condom to keep from leaving DNA evidence. He'd also worn gloves so there'd be no prints, a hat to keep his hair from shedding, and he'd shaved his pubes beforehand, which went to show premeditation.

"He told me he shaved for me, as a surprise, so I wouldn't get hair in my teeth!"

"Did you kill Wendy Abrams?"

"She's dead? The bitch is dead!? That's what this is about?!"

All Ronnie could scent was Mariah's hurt and anger, and it wasn't possible to be certain of whether she was telling the truth or not. However, it was clear she hadn't known her boyfriend had raped Wendy, which meant she probably hadn't killed her.

"Yes, someone killed her. We thought Jorge did, but now we aren't sure. He says she was alive when he was finished with her. We know she was killed the same night, likely sometime before daylight."

Her eyes narrowed. "If I could help you put him away, I would."

"I believe you. Are you okay? Do you need me to call someone for you?"

"No. Do I get a ride back home?"

"Up to you, but the ride home will be in a cop car."

She sighed and shook her head. "I'll call someone. Can I have my phone back?"

Procedure dictated Ronnie should leave, and then a deputy would show Mariah to the property area and return her things to her, but Ronnie had just given her horrible news, so she walked her to the property area and told them to turn her loose.

"I'm sorry I had to give you bad news, but now you know."

"You ain't bad, for a smurf."

Ronnie grinned. "You'd think I'd at least get to be Smurfette."

She smiled, and Ronnie turned and made the trek back to her murder room.

Everyone was back at their desks, and Agent Graham sat on the other side of Carter's desk. The two seemed to have hit it off.

She looked to Myers' desk, just outside her office door. "I saw notes on the victim's boyfriend when I was in my office earlier. Give me a few minutes to look over them and we'll go talk to him." She looked at Agent Graham. "He'll know you talked to her before she was killed, and he may blame you. Mind if I take this one without you?"

"Not a problem. He can answer questions to your murder but not the bribery case." He sat back, trying to look casual and put her at ease, which only put her on alert. "Our bosses have been talking over our heads about Flores and Ramirez. I asked to be the one to tell you, even though it wasn't my decision."

She sighed. "Yeah, I kinda thought they might. You're getting them for everything, aren't you?"

"Afraid so. The cases are tied together so tightly, it makes sense to handle them in one trial instead of two. This was the prosecutors making a deal over our heads. However, I've convinced my boss to let you keep them another twenty-four hours, in case you need to question them again for your murder case."

"I appreciate that, and in the end, as long as they're put away, that's the important part."

He stood, stepped forward, and offered his hand. "It was a pleasure working with you. I've made sure your men have everything I could get on Mick Griffin. I'll send one of my agents with you to clear the way with Griffin's bosses, but you're probably right about me not showing my face."

Ronnie shook his hand. "Thank you. If there's anything we can help you with in the future, let us know."

She watched him leave, and turned towards her office.

"The boyfriend's clean at first glance," said Detective Carter from behind her, "but Graham got us some inner-office data that shows he's been to anger management classes seven times in the thirteen years he's worked for the post office."

"He teaches Sunday School at his Baptist Church," said Sergeant Perry. "He's assistant coach over the church's youth baseball team, and he plays for the men's team. He's divorced, with only supervised visitation of his own kids, so I have to wonder why he's being trusted with the kids at church."

"I wonder how he feels about Halloween," Ronnie said. "Someone take a look at the church's website and see if they had an activity for the kids Saturday night, please, and whether they call it Halloween or a Fall Festival."

Ronnie sat at her desk and looked over the file. The suspect's given name was Micah Griffin, and he was certainly big enough to have carried Wendy to the zombie display — six four, two hundred and ten pounds. The full body shot of him looked more like a basketball player than a baseball player. His DMV photo made him look angry, while he appeared friendly in his post office ID shot. Go figure.

Both made him look pious.

If he killed her at work, this would end up being Graham's case, too.

But that wasn't likely.

Ronnie considered every angle, and decided she didn't want to question him at work, but she also didn't want to wait. She wanted to see his anger up close and personal — piss him off good and see what came out. He had a concealed carry license, but he couldn't carry at work, so it was the logical place to pick him up.

She hooked a body cam to her suit jacket, and instructed Henderson and Myers to do so as well.

She looked to the FBI agent. "If you can clear the way for us without alerting him, we'll be along about ten minutes after you."

He nodded and left, and she turned back to her men. "The passport office is just inside the main door of the post office. Henderson, you'll walk into the passport office with me. Myers, I want you inside the post office, but around the corner so Griffin can't look out and see you. Everyone else — go back to the cases you were working on before we landed Wendy's case."

"LT." This from Carter. He knew his Lieutenant took Henderson when she didn't want to intimidate a suspect. Henderson, in his snazzy suits, looked like a runway model. No way would a six foot two inch athlete with a black belt in two different disciplines see Henderson and a small female as a threat.

Her men knew her too well, but that didn't mean she was going to change things up. Henderson might not look like a badass, but he could hold his own, and so could she.

"We'll be fine," she assured them. "Myers will be right outside the door in case there's a problem. Ya'll want to make me happy? Get me at least one case cleared by the time I return."

The three rode in Henderson's car, and Ronnie ordered a squad car to keep close, so he could transport the suspect if he didn't come willingly. She read through the reports of what had been found in the car, and looked through the pictures. With the seat down, there was a decent amount of room to move around. They found hair that wasn't hers, but it wouldn't prove anything if it was her boyfriend's.

"The car doesn't help," she said. "We need to figure out how he got from the strip mall home."

"I've been working on that," said Henderson. "I haven't found anything yet. We need his phone records."

"We don't have enough to convince a judge." Henderson pulled into the post office parking lot and slid into a parking space. She unfastened her seatbelt. "Let's see what we can do about that, shall we?"

When Ronnie and Henderson walked into the passport office, Mick Griffin was behind the counter, talking to a woman across the counter about what her signature meant, and why she wanted to be sure everything was accurate.

Three people sat on benches, waiting.

"Micah Griffin?"

He glared at her. "If you have an appointment, please sit and wait until you're called."

This man had also been in Wendy's bedroom. Ronnie recognized his scent. He was her boyfriend, so it didn't mean he'd killed her, but she'd only smelled two men in that bedroom.

She wore her badge on a lanyard, and she lifted it to be sure he saw it, but kept her friendly smile. She was certain this video was going to be important, so her actions needed to be impeccable. "I'm Lieutenant Woods, with the

Hamilton County Sheriff's Office, Mr. Griffin. We need you to come downtown for questioning in the murder of Wendy Abrams."

He froze, and the scent of terror filled the room. Not fear. *Terror.*

Ronnie looked to the people waiting for their passports. "I'm terribly sorry about this. I don't know if someone else can come fill in for Mr. Griffin or not, but he might have information that can help us figure out who murdered his girlfriend, so he's going to have to come with us. If I can ask ya'll to step outside while we work through the logistics with him?"

Everyone moved to leave, and he said, "No! They're just local cops. I'm a *federal* employee. My orders trump theirs. Stay."

His last word was given as an order. Two of the customers hesitated, but Ronnie shook her head at them and they all filed out.

"You can't take me in! I'm a federal employee! You have no right! I'm a man of God! An upstanding citizen!"

"Which is why you should come with us willingly, Mr. Griffin. Any fine, upstanding citizen should want to help law enforcement find the man who killed his girlfriend."

She walked around the desk and into his space. "Let's go, sir. You can ride with us, and we'll bring you back when we're finished."

He stepped forward and looked down, trying to intimidate her. "I'll be more than happy to come in after my shift ends at 4:00, but my work here is *important*, and you won't interrupt it."

Ronnie lost her smile and stepped in closer, invading his space. "Murder trumps passports in the whole *importance* game, Mr. Griffin. You can come willingly or in handcuffs, totally up to you."

She saw the arm snake around and knew what he was about to do, and decided to let him. Her inner tiger understood her plan, and she, too, stayed silent and watched.

Micah Griffin proved how much of an asshole he was by nearly breaking her neck in a choke-hold. Clearly, the anger management classes hadn't worked.

If she'd been human, there's a good chance he'd have killed her.

Ronnie held her hand up — the signal to Henderson that she was fine and didn't need rescuing. She made sure Griffin held her for a count of three, to be sure Henderson's bodycam got a shot clear enough to grab a still shot, and then it was time to move.

She elbowed his ribs, flipped him up and over, and he should've landed on his back, but the bastard twisted in mid-air, landed on his feet, and punched her square in the face.

Again, she saw it coming, but with the video rolling it was important she was human-slow. His huge fist struck her jaw and cheek all at once. He rang her bell, but not her inner tiger's. Ronnie punched him hard enough the bastard took four steps back to keep from falling, a priceless look of surprised shock on his face.

While he was off balance, Ronnie swept his legs, rode him to the ground so he landed on his stomach, and finally cuffed him.

She stood and faced Henderson. "Subject is neutralized."

"I see that." His look clearly told her he had more to say, but would wait until the cameras weren't recording to do so. He looked down. "Sir? Mr. Griffin? Deputy Myers and I are going to help you stand."

Myers had stepped in when the commotion started, and Ronnie turned away while they helped Griffin up. A few deep breaths and she had her adrenaline response under control. When she turned back to them, they had him standing, and his gaze slammed into hers.

Didn't matter, he was her prisoner now — he'd just given her a reason for his initial arrest.

"Micah Griffin, you're under arrest for assaulting a police officer. You have the right to remain silent..."

Chapter Fourteen

Ronnie called the prosecutor on the way back to the station to see if she had enough for a warrant to search his house.

"What are we looking for?"

"The murder weapon, or anything else that might prove he killed his girlfriend."

She laughed. "Tell your men to get with Corey and get me a better list, and I'll see what I can do. Assaulting an officer when told you wanted to question him *might* be enough, but…" She blew out a breath. "You already know I can't get one because your gut says he did it." A pause. "It's enough to get my attention, though. Why is it always the husband or boyfriend? It's enough to make a girl stay single."

Candace Blevins

Ronnie could've stepped into the bathroom, managed a partial *change*, and fixed her face, but she needed her jaw and cheek to flower into a full bruise. She popped a few aspirin to help move things along, because her shapeshifter genes would make her heal faster even if she didn't *change*.

When she walked into her murder room, her men had her little scuffle with Griffin playing on a continuous loop. She rolled her eyes and made a beeline for her office, but *Eye of the Tiger* started playing, and she couldn't help but smile. "Get back to work! Henderson, Myers, Corey — in my office!"

"He played football and baseball in high school," Corey told her when he walked in. "Worked a number of odd jobs before taking the exam to work for the federal government at twenty-one. He went to work for the post office, sorting. He was married six months later, divorced three years later with one child, and his wife pregnant with another. Griffin roughed her up at six months pregnant, put her in the hospital. She filed for divorce before she was even released from the hospital, along with a request for a restraining order, which was dropped before it made in front of a judge."

"How does he have a carry license with domestic violence charges?"

"Nothing stuck."

"Where does the ex-wife work?"

"She's remarried. Works for her husband. He's an artist and she's his manager."

Ronnie blew out a breath. She might learn something from the ex-wife, but probably nothing immediately useful, and Ronnie needed to get to this guy before he came to his senses and lawyered up.

"Okay, so he has supervised visitation for his own kids, but he's in charge of other people's kids at church. Did he ever marry again?"

"No. Looking through social media, he's only been at this church two years, and he left his last church because it was *no longer a good fit.*"

Ronnie immediately knew she needed to talk to that pastor to find out what'd gone wrong. Corey read her face and set a piece of paper down with the name of the church, the name of the pastor, and a phone number.

It took a few minutes to get him on the phone, and Ronnie dove straight in. "Pastor Davis. I'm Lieutenant Woods with the Hamilton County Sheriff's Office, and I'd like to ask you some questions about Mick Griffin. I won't take up much of your time, and I hate to do this over the phone, but I just need a quick rundown of why he left your church and started going to another, please."

"I don't like to speak badly of any of God's children."

"I understand, sir, but I'm trying to establish a pattern, so even if you just hit the high spots, it will help me immensely."

"When we reorganized our youth division, we had too many Sunday school teachers, and so he was no longer needed. Also, our new youth director became assistant coach to a retired schoolteacher who'd coached for a local high school, so we didn't need Mick's help there, either."

Ronnie read between the lines. They'd had problems and needed to get him away from the kids, but the preacher wasn't going to libel himself by giving her the details. That was okay for the time being. It gave her a starting point.

"Okay, Pastor. I may need to talk to you in person and hear more details than you're willing to give right now, but you've confirmed a suspicion. One more thing, if you can tell me when he joined your church, and which church he'd come from?"

"I can do that. Give me just a minute."

He must've put her on hold, because she heard nothing for a moment, and then a woman picked up and gave her the dates and previous church. Ronnie wrote them down, did the math in her head, and realized he'd only been at that church a year and a half.

"There's something else, Ma'am."

The woman sounded hesitant, and she spoke softly. Ronnie's hackles went up, but she merely said, "Yes? What else?"

"He went to Cancun with a girl he met at church, and she died while they were on vacation. Was found floatin' in the swimmin' pool. The Mexican police ruled it a drownin', and since she didn't have no family, she was cremated down there, so no one would have to pay to ship her home."

"Thank you for that information. It isn't in any of my paperwork because it happened outside the country. What's your name, Ma'am?"

Ronnie got her information, hung up, and turned to Corey. "How do we even *try* to find information about women he left the country with who didn't make it home?" While he considered the question, she lifted her phone and called Perry's extension.

"Are you deep into something?"

"What do you need?"

She told him what she'd found, and he said, "You need me to keep following the trail back, see what churches he went to, and find someone gossipy at each church to give me dirt."

"Yes, please."

She saw him push away from his desk as he said, "I'm on it. I'll phone anything big I get into Corey."

"Thanks, Sergeant."

Ronnie sensed a change in the room, and saw Commander Frost marching through her murder room. She stood when he entered her office.

"Commander."

"Lieutenant. When are you going to let the men handle the bad guys?"

She rolled her eyes and grinned. "He killed her, Sir. Now I just have to prove it."

"Gut, or do you have something tangible?"

"Motive, means, and opportunity."

He lifted an eyebrow and she rolled her eyes. "I'm going on my gut again, Sir. *Please* tell me you aren't going to keep me out of the box?"

"No, we need you in there, but you can't be alone with him."

"He'll be handcuffed, and I took care of him the first time, I'll take care of him again if he acts up."

"And you'll piss him off to get a reaction, right? He's going to act up again because you'll make sure he does."

She grinned and shrugged. "Whatever works, Sir."

He sat in a chair across from her, and she sat, too.

"Tell me."

It was an order, and she went through what she knew and what she assumed, and pointed out she wanted to get to him sooner rather than later, and not let him stew so long he asked for his lawyer. He stood with a nod.

"You think it's more than the two women?"

"There's a damned good chance. I'm going to try to nail him on Wendy Abrams today, but we're going to have to dig to see what else we can find."

"Okay. Let's work on getting enough for a search warrant. I assume you have someone sitting on his house to make sure no one cleans it out for him?"

She nodded, he nodded, and he was gone.

Chapter Fifteen

Ronnie walked into the interrogation room and met the gaze of her pissed-off murder suspect, dressed in orange, with a black eye blossoming on his left side. His cheek didn't look so good either. She hoped she hadn't broken it, but the video would exonerate her of any claims he made about police brutality.

Her own cheek was blossoming as well, but she'd put makeup on so he wouldn't see. They needed pictures for court, but he didn't need the satisfaction of knowing he'd hurt her. Myers stood just inside the door, and she hoped Griffin thought it was just policy.

"I read you your rights, and I'm sure they did so again when they booked you. Do you understand them?"

"Yes, and I still don't understand why I'm here!"

An absolute lie, but she decided not to point it out.

"Where were you on the night of October thirtieth?"

"The church held a Fall Festival on the thirty-first, and I manned the pumpkin trebuchet. Our youth built three of them, and then competed to see who could get their pumpkins the farthest. The night before, I was at the church helping them with the final touches on their trebuchets."

"How late were you there?"

"I believe I arrived home around ten. Wendy was supposed to help with the cotton candy machine the next night, but she totally skipped out on us without so much as a phone call." He sighed. "I was so mad, I didn't even call to check on her, and then I felt guilty about being mad at her once I found out she'd been killed."

Another lie, but it wasn't time to call him on it just yet.

"So, you left the church before ten o'clock on the thirtieth. Did you go to Wendy's house? Or did she come to your house? Had ya'll had sex? I bet you were *pissed* when you found out she'd screwed someone else."

He stared at his hands, and Ronnie kept going. "Not only that, but she had the evil, *perverted* kind of sex with him, when she was supposed to be clean, for *you*! It was like she pissed all over everything the two of you had!"

He shook his head and kept staring at his hands. "I don't know what you're talking about."

Another lie, but Ronnie could almost smell the outburst just under his skin.

"All those nights you were so hard you *hurt*, but you held off, and she goes and gives it up for a *stranger*, and then has the nerve to cry and act like she's the victim, and not you!"

"I was going to ask her to marry me! She'd done penance for her sins, for having sex out of wedlock when she was younger, but she'd been celibate for over two years! And then she lay with someone else! She was unclean!"

"So you had to *help* her get clean, didn't you!"

"I did! The bible says a woman should be stoned to death, but I figured bullets are the modern-day equivalent, and..." He sighed. "Where would I have even found stones big enough, that late at night?"

Ronnie glanced at the camera, and Corey knew what she was thinking. "Commander Frost is on the phone about the warrant, Lieutenant." Ronnie wanted to look over the list of items before it was submitted, but she had to trust her people.

"So, walk me through this," she told the murdering bastard across the table. "Did you drop by her house? Find her crying?"

He must've realized he'd just screwed himself, because he shut down. "I need my lawyer."

"Yes, sir. I believe you're right about that."

Ronnie stood and walked out of the room without looking back. Looked like she was going to get to help create that list, after all.

She sat with her team, worked on the list of items they were looking for, and then called everyone into the conference room. Perry had returned after visiting two more churches, and Carter was back after talking to the ex-wife.

Commander Frost had the assistant DA stop by, and she told them, "We can't prosecute him for a crime in Cancun. If you want to try to track down every person he left the country with, we can probably make that happen with the FBI's help, but it sounds as if he only dated people with no family, until Wendy, anyway. There aren't going to be missing person's reports. No family or friends looking for closure."

"So you're saying there's no reason to find them?" Ronnie sighed. From the standpoint of what the department could do with limited funds, she had a point, but it stung. It was like saying those women didn't matter. However, spending resources on a crime they couldn't prosecute wasn't going to go over well with the brass.

She looked at her Commander. "I think we should follow the churches back, on the chance we find another murder that may have happened *here*."

"We're going to put him away for murder without doing that, Ronnie." He used her name, which meant this was a conversation and not him making an edict as Commander.

"Yes, Sir, we are. I'd still like to make sure there isn't something important we're missing. We *might* solve a cold case while we're at it — someone with family, before he learned to find people no one cared about."

He sighed. "Send your junior detectives out. I want your core team focused on making sure we have him dead to rights on *this* murder."

"Thank you, Commander."

Ronnie slid into her car at nearly six — earlier than normal, but she hoped to return after dark with a vampire who'd tell her every crime Mick Griffin had committed.

She texted Josef she was on her way, and he called her back on the encoded app she used to talk to Nathan about supernatural issues. She was glad most criminals hadn't figured this little trick out.

"*Bellula*. I hope you've had a productive day."

"Most would say I did. How are you this evening?" Her inner tiger yowled in annoyance, and Ronnie agreed. "Crap, sorry. I hate small talk and I was starting it. I don't know what to say to you. I mean, asking how you slept is stupid because it isn't sleep."

"I am *wonderful* this evening, with a smile on my face that's made everyone I've been on video chat with a nervous Nelly."

"Do you need me to bring anything? Should I grab something to eat before I come?"

"Please don't. I enjoy feeding you."

"Okay, and I tried not to feel awkward last night, but it's odd, eating when you aren't."

"I've already fed this evening. I will drink wine with you."

"Is it rude for me to ask how you pick your meals? Do you have someone who stays there?"

"At different times in my life, I have different options. A team of wolves is nearly always close at hand when I awaken, and I'm welcome to any of them. Abbott often sends a breakfast treat, someone from his flock. I occasionally hunt for my own food, when I want a specific flavor or energy, or I'm just in the mood to hunt."

She wanted to ask how often he had sex when he fed, but it seemed rude.

Before she could think of something else to say, he told her, "Your Amakhosi paid me a visit shortly after I awakened."

She sighed. "I'm sorry. He was waiting for me when I arrived home this morning."

"No need to apologize. As I told him, one usually only has to check in with him before engaging in a friendship — or more — with one of his lionesses. He agreed with me, and there wasn't a problem. He gave me the green light, with the usual threats should I harm a single hair on your head, or cause you an ounce of emotional pain."

She laughed through her embarrassment. "I really am sorry. He's a little over-protective, sometimes."

"Having the Amakhosi protecting you is a good thing, *Bellula*. I'm glad you have people in your life who love you."

Love? Did Nathan love her? Yes, she supposed he did, but it wasn't romantic. Not really fatherly, either. He was her King — her Liege — and she loved him, but she'd never considered his reciprocation, which was silly, in retrospect. He took time to keep up with her life, and he showed up at her house when he discovered she was involved with a powerful vampire. Of *course* these things showed he cared about her as a person and not merely a subject.

"I suppose you're right. I have my team at work, the friends I was with the other night, Nathan, and even his primary Pride. I mean, I'm not part of the Pride, but I feel close to the women."

"And your family?"

She sighed. "That's *much* too deep a subject for our evening."

"When you are ready to share it with me, I shall listen."

After a few seconds of uncomfortable silence, he said, "Martin has never expected people to come to him before forming a relationship with one of his tigers. I'm assuming this is still the case?"

"Yes. I'm Martin's tiger, but since Nathan is king of *all* cats, I also belong to him."

"Okay, *Bellula*. One of my wolves will bring you to me when you arrive. I regret that I cannot meet you aboveground."

She took a breath. "Are you still open to helping me with my investigation?"

129

"I am. Please don't sound so nervous about asking. I told you — I wish to see this case come to a satisfying conclusion."

"That isn't likely, but he'll at least spend the rest of his life in prison, I hope."

"You hope?"

"Yes. As it stands now, he might get out when he's an old man. I need help making sure he comes out in a bodybag."

"Then I shall help you."

"I'm pulling into your neighborhood. I'll let you go. See you in a few minutes."

Josef lived on a different road than the coterie house, but if he went through the backyards, he was actually quite close. A female werewolf met her in the driveway and motioned her to pull into the six-car garage.

It didn't escape Ronnie's notice that the doors leading downstairs were open before she came into the living room. He wasn't ready for her to know how to open those doors, which was understandable. The *old ones* didn't get that way by taking chances with their hidey-holes.

The door was under a beautiful staircase, which made sense, as this staircase led down. They stepped onto a landing without an exit, the wolf put her hand on a palm reader, and another door opened. The next door, however, must've been another old-fashioned secret-mechanism door, because it was open, with a male werewolf guarding it.

Josef had chosen to utilize technology, but he didn't completely trust it. Every other door was old-school and then modern tech. Again — *interesting*.

At last, they came to a solid wall, and the wolf told her, "When I'm gone, telepath him that you're outside his chamber, and alone."

She climbed six steps, and a wall formed four steps up, so Ronnie was alone in a room with zero light. Even her tiger vision was useless.

Josef? I'm here and it's dark. I wish you'd warned me.

Her physical body was on full alert, but Ronnie was pissed instead of scared. The cat stood inside her and took note, annoyed, but not angry.

The wall opened, light spilled in, and Josef stood before her, so poised she wanted to punch him.

"I apologize, *Bellula*. The final room is kind of my own personal Rubicon. I hope you'll forgive an old vampire his eccentricities."

"You haven't given me bullshit before, don't start now. You can find out a lot about a person's intent in that dark room, can't you?"

He smiled. "You've reminded me once again why I'm so enraptured with you, *Bellula*. Straight to the point. Yes, you are absolutely correct."

His eyes went sharp and within a microsecond he'd closed the distance between them. She jerked her chin at his touch, but he held it steady, cupping it, his fingers firm.

"Increase light." His voice was sharp, no nonsense, and the lights in the room brightened.

"Your face is bruised. You're a fucking *tiger* and your face is bruised."

His voice was ice, his eyes cold. Ronnie didn't try to step away because to do so would be to admit he'd alarmed her.

"I'm a cop. Sometimes the bad guys don't want me to put cuffs on them. It happens."

He didn't say anything. He merely stood like a statue, motionless, holding her chin, his icy gaze on the bruise.

"I popped a few aspirins to make sure the bruise formed. We got lots of pictures before I left work, because we initially brought him in for assaulting an officer. We have him on murder now, but we need to make sure the first charge holds or the second could fall apart."

He finally let go of her chin. "I can fry his brain from the inside, and no one will know what happened."

She shook her head. "Not while he's in our custody, Josef. You have to promise. It looks bad on *me* when people come into my custody healthy and don't leave the same way."

"Later, then."

"No! You can't fry the brain of everyone who punches me!"

"Can't I?"

She crossed her arms and glared at him.

Josef sighed. "Yes, okay. He's *your* prisoner, and the bruise will heal. Come, your meal is ready."

They walked through a maze of rooms Ronnie was certain was also part of his security, and ended up in a dining room. She didn't ask why a vampire had a dining room table and a kitchen in his downstairs lair.

But her mouth watered and her inner tigress rose up, sniffing.

He'd made her a bison pot roast in the biggest crock pot she'd ever seen.

"You cook?"

"I started it in the upstairs kitchen before dawn this morning, and asked my wolves to keep an eye on it. They brought it down once I awakened. I've chosen a robust wine, from vineyards I own in Italy. I hope you find it goes well with the bison."

Another thing about the *old ones*. If they aren't disgustingly rich, they're doing something very wrong.

"Thank you, for taking the time and effort to feed me." She took a breath. "Traditionally, this requires—"

"Fuck tradition," he interrupted. "You aren't obligated to feed me. I'll be thrilled if you wish to, someday, but I'll have to see into your head enough to be certain you aren't doing it out of a misplaced sense of right and wrong." He caressed her bruised cheek, a whisper of a touch. "I won't drink from you unless it's for the right reasons, and it could be one of a hundred right reasons, but it should be intimate and special. It should bring us closer together. If it won't do those things, I'll wait until it will."

She told him about her day while she ate. At first, he wasn't amused when he discovered she'd goaded the man into striking her, but then he'd changed his mind, as if he understood the strategy and respected it.

When she finished the story, he sat back and steepled his fingers, considering. "Give me two hours with him, and I'll give him nightmares. I'll force him to relive every murder he's committed, but from the perspective of the person who died — and I've been inside people's heads when they died, I *know* how to show him the feeling. When he awakens, he'll ask for a paper and pen so he can detail every single murder."

"You're sure you can do this?"

"If he's too strong for suggestions, I'll speak to him in his head and claim to be God. I'll tell him he'll have the same nightmare every night until he confesses."

"No. If he starts talking about God in his head, the psychiatrists will get involved and everything'll go to shit. I want him in *prison*."

"I'll make the suggestion work, and he won't speak to anyone of *why* he's choosing to confess. It might not happen right when he awakens, though. Depends on how strong his willpower is, and how much of a sociopath he is."

"How close do you need to be from the jail?"

He hesitated a brief moment. "I can reach the county jail from our downtown billiard club."

Ronnie sat back. "My office is in the same block."

"Yes. I've stayed out of your head, Ronnie."

He smelled of the truth, but the *old ones* knew how to mask their scent when they lied. She'd have to believe him until he gave her reason not to, though.

"He had a small cut near his eye — a side effect of me ramming my fist into it. I wiped my hand on my shirt. I've changed clothes since then, but I have it in a sealed bag, if that will help you find his mind inside the jail."

"His location inside the jail is more important at this point. His blood will be dead by now, so I can't use it to find him." He gave her an appraising look before adding, "I need to tell you that I'm restricted about what I can share with you — certain details about my kind that aren't commonly known. I'm treading terribly close to the line."

"Please don't do anything to get yourself in hot water. If there's anything I can do to lift those restrictions, please let me know."

Chapter Sixteen

She'd have to let him feed from her before Abbott let him talk more freely, and no way in hell was Josef telling her that.

His little tiger asked to use his shower when she finished eating, but he didn't point out that doing so wouldn't wash the smell of the Amakhosi from her. The Lion King hadn't had sex with her, but he'd still managed to get his scent all over her. Josef got the message loud and clear —Veronica Woods was under Nathan's protection, and Josef was taking his life in his hands if he didn't treat her right.

Not a problem, since he intended to treat her better than any princess in history.

Though the bruise on her cheek was damned hard to look at, and not killing the bastard who did it seemed wrong, but he understood why he couldn't bring physical harm to him.

Emotional pain, though — that was fair game.

His *Bellula* came out of the bathroom in nothing but a towel, and she *stalked* him. The tiger wasn't far below the surface, and he let her climb on his lap. He sat on an oversized sofa, and she pushed him sideways, so he was lying on his back, the tiger riding him. He let his cock fill, and he pulled her down to him.

He had no idea what'd brought this on, but he wasn't arguing. He pulled her to him, but she shook her head and sat back up, riding him, her bare pussy over his slacks, his cock *throbbing*. She unbuttoned his shirt, spread it open, traced his abs. Finally, his little tigress scooted back enough to unfasten his belt and trousers. She looked at her hand and it transformed into a paw, and she flexed it until the claws were out, but Josef didn't move to defend himself. If she hurt him, he'd heal, but she might never recover from him not trusting her.

She sliced his underwear off him, turned her paw back into a hand, and moved to sit on his cock, but that was asking too much.

Josef needed to be in control the first time he entered his *Bellula*. He flipped her over so he was on top, and her heart heart skipped and faltered, but he kissed her until it raced again.

No, he didn't kiss her, he devoured her taste, her heartbeat, her scent, her heat. He moved down her body, kissed her nipples, sucked one into his mouth, then the other, and was careful his fangs didn't extend.

Ronnie couldn't handle being on the bottom, but Josef overwhelmed her senses so much, she wasn't capable of protesting. No one ever fucked *her* — she was always on top. Always in control. *She screwed them, not the other way around.*

However, when he moved down her body and worshiped her with his mouth, she could convince herself she was in control and he was doing her bidding, though in her heart, she knew it wasn't the case. He was controlling this ride, but his mouth felt so damned *good*. His tongue, his lips, even his teeth — his very dull, human teeth. She wasn't in the least bit worried about him biting her. Nathan would have his head if Josef bit her when she hadn't given him leave.

Josef lifted over her to enter her, and at the last second, she took him by surprise and flipped them over again. They landed on the carpeted floor with her on top, and she sat onto him with a groan, taking him into her and accepting him inside her body on *her* terms, but he used her momentum and kept them going, so he was on top a half-second later. He sucked a nipple in while he hit a magical spot inside she hadn't known existed, and her entire body went limp with pleasure.

Josef moved, in and out, so smooth, so assured. He hit the *magical spot* every time, over and over until a storm gathered inside her — too much pleasure, too much heat.

"Don't. I can't. I *can't*."

He went in and held. Ran his free hand over her thigh, soothing her. He released her nipple from his lips and met her gaze. "Your scent says yes, why does your mouth say you can't?"

He went out and back in. The head of his cock scraped deliciously over *the spot*, and her damned eyes rolled into the back of her head.

"I can't. *Please*."

"You *are*, Ronnie. I choose to believe your scent, and your reactions."

He lifted her legs into the air, his hands stroked her legs, his cock moved across the magical place inside her, and her eyes lost focus, the room went hazy.

"Release your shield for me. Let me see."

It was an order, but she shook her head. She wouldn't. *Couldn't.*

"You want sex without the connection? They make battery powered toys for that. You have *me*, little tiger. Open your eyes and see me."

His gaze slammed into hers, and he was right. It was Josef. Not the monster. She'd killed the monster. This was *Josef.*

"Let go of whatever demons you refuse to show me. Don't let them win. It's just the two of us in this room. No one else is invited. *Look at me.* Let me give you pleasure. I won't take it. *Let me.*"

He asked instead of demanding, and it changed everything. *Everything.*

Her pulse throbbed in her throat. Her heart raced. She didn't realize her breath was ragged until she tried to talk again. "Permission. Okay. Follow scent."

Ronnie hoped to hell he understood she wanted him to follow her scent and not what she said, and he seemed to, because he grasped her hands and held them over her head, and moved inside her with purpose, as if his new goal in life was her pleasure.

Now, he moved over her and destroyed her. His gaze, his cock, the magical spot inside her, and then his free hand pressed the area around her clit, and pleasure engulfed her, hot and vicious, a wave of passion so intense she couldn't breathe.

Intense pleasure gripped her, held her. When it finally released her, Ronnie's body went limp, scrambled thoughts a blur, but Josef lifted her and settled her chest and stomach on the sofa, her legs hanging down and her knees on the carpet. He entered her again, so thick and fat inside her, spreading her open again. Entering. Invading. Owning.

"Motherfucker! I can't again. *Please.*" The last word came out as a sob. He'd destroy her if he made her orgasm so out of control like that again.

"Not what your scent says, my darling *Bellula.*"

He moved behind her, one hand grasping her hair while another held her right wrist.

The tidal wave built inside her fast this time, as if it'd been waiting her entire life to burst forth, and her back arched to give him more room to work. This time, when she barreled over the peak and plummeted down the other side, it was as if her heart were laid bare and nothing protected it. Years of making sure she was in control and no one could ever hurt her again, and Josef had wiped it all away in moments. Another sob broke loose, and he pushed her onto the sofa, onto her back, and entered her again.

"Look at me. Wrap your legs around me, Ronnie. It's me. Focus, *Bellula*."

Her next orgasm tore through Josef and may as well have been her tigress claws. Had his little *Bellula* never had an orgasm? There was no time to think of the repercussions now, because he knew in his ancient vampire heart that if he didn't manage a big breakthrough now, she'd shut him out and that would be it. Something had hurt her — he'd known she had secrets, but had no idea how deep her secrets might lie.

He swept her through two more earthshattering orgasms, and his little tiger waited until he was emptying himself into her to open her shields and think of everything. No more secrets. In a matter of moments, he had the entire, horrible, gut-wrenching story.

Years of her father raping her, coming to her at night, forcing her into silence. Tired of his human wife, he wanted to fuck a tiger, and when his daughter started growing curves, he'd wanted her, so he'd taken her. Eight fucking years old, and he'd promised it was okay because she couldn't get pregnant since she hadn't started her period yet, but he'd guilted her into keeping the secret and not telling her mother or friends.

But he'd misjudged when her period would come — *and thus, when her tiger would first emerge. At twelve, with her inner tigress so close, she screamed and cursed at him for the first time, which had brought her mother to see what was the matter, and he'd killed his wife to keep her from calling nine-one-one.*

And it was at that moment little Veronica's tiger had chose to come out in physical form for the first time, and she'd killed her father. It'd been tiger against tiger, and the little one had eaten his heart. Her tiger had been born of blood, and yet she was a police officer, fighting for human justice, for human laws.

"I should leave."

She was still in his arms, still naked, but stiff as a board.

"Not an option. You will let me hold you because I need your warmth, and because you need my arms around you. We need each other right now. If you insist on leaving, I will call the Amakhosi and tell him to come get you because you can't be alone right now."

Josef remembered the incident from years ago — someone had brought Abbott into it for damage control, and he'd contacted Nathan. This was why the two were so close. Nathan had likely taken her in for a few nights while he found a feline family capable of handling her until she was grown. In all likelihood, Nathan had taught her how to control her inner tigress, and not Martin. Certainly not her father.

"You wouldn't!" She sighed and shook her head. "Look — we fucked, it's over."

"You don't believe that. Besides, don't you want to ride with me later, be there when I fuck with your prisoner's head?"

"You don't play fair."

"I'm not playing, but you're correct that I'll do whatever is necessary to stop a catastrophe, and you walking out my door right now would devastate me, and, I believe, you. You've put the shield back up so I don't know for certain, of course."

"You're…"

Josef slid a single finger inside her, and her eyes rolled back in her head, her heartbeat stuttered, and her scent… *damn*, her scent might very well do him in.

Chapter Seventeen

This time, Josef's *Bellula* came out of the shower in jeans, a thin sweater, and a sexy female version of modern-day army combat boots. Vampires have total control of every part of their body — even whether their heart beats or not — and yet his dick began to fill without him aiming extra blood flow to the area. He diverted the flow away with a tiny shake of his head. This woman spoke to him as no female had in centuries. No, farther back. Much farther back.

She was a strong warrior woman who wasn't afraid of *being* a woman. The warrior men she commanded respected her for it, as they might not have respected a woman trying to act like a man. He'd need to think on this, but not now.

Josef wore black fatigues and a black microfiber performance t-shirt. Abbott's second-in-command eschewed all modern fabrics, but Josef saw their purpose and appreciated them as a tool. Wars had been won and lost based on who had the most functional attire for the weather and terrain, and he would always think like a general.

He pulled his little tiger into his arms, and she curled contentedly into them as if they'd done it a thousand times. So comfortable, for such a new relationship.

"Thank you, for showing me. For letting me in. I know it wasn't easy." It occurred to him he hadn't let her know he was glad she'd shared it with him, and not dismayed.

She shook her head, her cheek scraping against his chest. "It's my past, not my present. Nathan warned me you wouldn't let me stay in control. I knew what I was getting into, but you had it right — I'm not a coward. I like you, and turning away because I was afraid wasn't an option."

He leaned back, touched under her chin, caressed the bruised cheek. "You've never had an orgasm?"

"I've had plenty of them, but I gave them to myself with either a toy or a man's cock. No one's ever *given* me an orgasm. It was hard, and it might be hard for a few more times, but it'll get easier." Her gaze met his, unwavering, resolute. Brave. She telepathed, *You touched me in places no one has.*

Josef felt a little like that ridiculous Christmas show, where the monster's heart grows three sizes larger. He pulled her to him and closed his eyes while raw emotion scraped him in places he'd forgotten could be vulnerable, deep, deep inside.

"Right back atcha, Lieutenant. I'm raw inside, and you've done it. My heart is yours, please don't break it."

She chuckled. "I'm raw inside, too. *Damn*, you can go forever."

"I know you can *change* and heal, but I quite like knowing you feel me inside, even now."

Josef chose the Maserati Quattroporte, not to impress her, but to be assured of her comfort. Their conversation was casual as he drove. He asked of her favorite food, and what she didn't like. She answered all his questions, and he wondered if she knew how long it'd been since he'd needed to ask these things. After some thought, it felt important to tell her.

"I haven't had to ask someone what they like to eat in so long, I can't remember when I last did so. I find I'm enjoying getting to know you this way. Anytime you want to give me more, I'm open to it, but I'm not complaining about learning of you by what you tell me. It's a little like slowly unwrapping a present."

"Maybe it's time for me to ask some questions? What do *you* like to eat? Do you prefer male or female? Wolf, human? Something else? Does the food they eat flavor their blood?"

"I consider the coterie's wolves mine, since they're part of our security team and I'm in charge of them, but really, everything belongs to Abbott." He shrugged. "The point is, I feed from my wolves so frequently, a change to a different shapeshifter is nice. I rarely feed from humans these days — shapeshifters give so much more of their life force. Abbott's flock is fed a specific menu, so their blood always tastes exceptionally good. My wolves have a list of forbidden foods, but they're allowed to eat as they wish on a rotating cycle. We have enough, they aren't always on the menu."

"Which foods?"

He shook his head. He wasn't going to make her feel as if she shouldn't eat garlic or asparagus. Not many people liked cooked cabbage or Brussels sprouts these days, so those items weren't usually a problem.

"Fine. Don't tell me about the food, but you didn't answer the male or female question."

Spoken like a skilled interrogator. He was rapidly falling for this woman.

No, he'd already fallen for her.

"It depends upon my mood. I enjoy both, for different reasons." He sighed. He didn't have to dig into her mind to know where her questions were leading. "Ask what you *really* want to know, please."

"It's none of my business."

She didn't know it yet, but her life was now his business, and his life was going to be hers. He answered even though she hadn't asked.

"I can feed without the fucking part, but I don't often do so. Sometimes, Abbott sends a 'feed only' treat, and I don't push for more. A few of the coterie wolves don't like being fucked by me, so when they come up on the schedule, I only feed from them because I'm not a monster."

Unless there was an attitude problem and it was necessary, but that was a different conversation. He glanced at her and looked back to the road. "I wish I knew what you're thinking, but I won't go back on my word, so I'm not looking."

"Tigers aren't especially monogamous, but I find I'm envious of whoever you'll screw tomorrow when you awaken." A sigh. "I'm not asking you not to have sex with them, but you're nice enough not to look, so it seemed I should tell you."

He sensed a sudden question — something she'd just thought of — a microsecond before she asked, "You screw the men *and* women? No, don't answer that, of course you do. I remember someone telling me the long-lived are almost all bisexual."

"I believe the modern term is pan, and yes, I am. Is that a problem?"

"No, not at all, it was just a surprise, until I considered it."

"I won't fuck anyone else for the near future, at least until we figure out whatever is happening between us."

"I didn't ask that of you."

"I know, but it feels important. We need to figure *us* out. The spark got us started, but now we have to…" He caressed her cheek. "Like someone weaving a tapestry, we must weave the details of our lives into a single image. How it looks is entirely up to us."

"*Fuck*, I work with a bunch of human detectives. I can't date a vampire!"

Right, because eventually, they'd realize they only saw him at night, and would try to create reasons for him to show up during the day. Detectives have to pick at the unknown. It's who they are.

"Not a problem," he assured her. "Abbott and Kendra are better at long term adjustments. I can ask them to make sure no one who works with you will wonder why they never see me during the day, and will never do a deep background check. It's solid, and will hold up to scrutiny, but your men might smell something just because they're so good at their jobs."

"I want to forbid you from screwing with their heads, but I know that isn't realistic. Nothing yet, though. Okay?"

Ronnie's cop instincts went on alert at the two unknown men on the balcony when Josef pulled into the back parking lot of The Billiard Club at close to one in the morning. She opened her door and stood to get a better look, her hand close to her weapon because strange men in an alley might mean problems. Her gaze met that of a gorgeous vampire. His companion was a werewolf, and just as beautiful. She breathed out and relaxed. They belonged here.

Josef exited the car slower than her. "I'm more than capable of protecting you, should it be necessary, though it isn't this evening." He walked her up the steps and introduced everyone. "Lieutenant Veronica Woods, meet The Abbott and Spencer. Abbott, Spence, this is Ronnie."

"It's nice to finally make your acquaintance," said Abbott. "We've been most curious about you." He eyed Josef. "This is a woman who will never wait for someone to rescue her. She might call for a pickup after she's slaughtered those who mean her harm, or perhaps arrested them if they're human, but I don't think the protective knight thing is going to work with her."

"What he means to say," said Spencer, "is that Josef *never* falls head over heels, and we've been dying to meet you. Have you eaten? The kitchen's about to close — want to help me eat whatever was cooked and not ordered? There are always appetizers at the end of the night."

"No, thank you. Josef is quite good at keeping me fed."

"And I have a task to complete for her," Josef told them, "so I'm going to have to disappoint you by squirreling her away with me in a sleeping room a few hours."

After about ten seconds, Abbott looked at Ronnie with a new understanding. They'd been telepathing, apparently. "Ah. I see. Well, I look forward to getting to know you better another time."

Ronnie looked up to Josef, who seemed uncomfortable, and then to Abbott. "Nathan visited Josef yesterday, it seems *both* our respective hierarchies feel the need to meddle. I'm glad Josef has people who care for him. I don't know what kind of gathering we can plan for the two of you as well as Nathan and possibly Martin, but I'll try to make something happen in the next two weeks."

"That will be wonderful," said Spence. "Let me know what I can do to help, please. Drinks with hors d'oeuvres would be appropriate. I can help with the menu."

Spence was so beautiful, he nearly took her breath away, but she didn't want him. She only wanted Josef. "That would be nice. Thank you."

Once they were inside, Josef telepathed. *It's best we keep Nathan and Abbott out of the same room.*

Crap, how could she have forgotten? The two had negotiated a truce of sorts, but a friendly visit was asking too much.

I somehow forgot he was that *Abbott. I mean, I knew, but it didn't all come together in my head. Okay then, Martin and Abbott at one gathering, and then just Nathan for another.*

I don't know. If we manage it with care, we might bring the two of them back to a working relationship. Let me think on it.

Chapter Eighteen

Josef settled her overnight bag on a table in a secure sleeping room, and she pulled shorts and a shirt out.

"You'll need more covering you," he told her. "If we're both to be under the covers. I'll leach too much of your heat away."

"It's what I brought. I sleep hot, usually. We'll see how it goes."

She went to the restroom to change, and he was nude and under the covers when she returned. He'd pulled the sealed bag with her shirt out, and he opened it and smelled. There was no magic, but scent gave off an energy, and it couldn't hurt to familiarize himself with the man in any way easily possible. He also looked over the rough-drawn map of the block showing where the jail was again, and then the rough sketch of the jail, with an asterisk showing where he was. She'd informed him it was her best drawing of an asshole.

He'd never again see an asterisk without thinking of how it resembled an asshole.

Ronnie curled into him, and he wrapped an arm around her. He wanted her to be comfortably asleep before he started. Thankfully, she was exhausted so it didn't take long.

He'd found his target while she found sleep, and once her breathing evened out, it was time to get to work.

Mick Griffin was also asleep, which helped matters, but Josef still felt the rancid, oily residue of malevolence and even evil while he probed the asshole's memories.

Mick had made his first kill two days after his wife had filed for divorce — a young runaway selling herself on the street. He'd made sure no one would miss her before he'd killed her, and he hadn't even bothered to find out her name. He'd known *Candy* was a street name, and not real. He'd buried her in his backyard while his wife was in the hospital, and had installed a patio over the top of the grave the next day.

It took longer than two hours for Josef to dig through Griffin's memory and be sure he'd found every murder. Seventeen women.

Josef chose three to make the evil motherfucker live through, and made sure he paralyzed the bastard's body, so his thrashing and fighting wouldn't attract anyone's attention. Josef put him through hell three fucking times — right to the point of death, his body starved for oxygen in two cases, blood in another, at the point of losing consciousness.

Finally, Josef put the suggestion in Griffin's head that he'd have nightmares for the rest of his life, cycling through his victims every time he slept, until he confessed. The only way to keep from living what they'd felt, over and over, night after night, was to confess every crime. Josef woke him up, had him relieve himself and shake the dreams off, and then put him back to sleep so he could make him experience two more murders. When the dawn grew close, Josef left a note for Ronnie, and moved into a secure resting compartment before the dawn took him.

Chapter Nineteen

Ronnie awakened to her cellphone alarm and instantly missed Josef's cool strength in bed beside her. He'd worried about leaching her heat, but in truth, she slept better with him beside her — like holding onto chilled granite, so she slept cool and not so hot.

She changed into slacks and a silk t-shirt, put her holster belt on, weaponed up, and slid into her dress shoes. As promised, a werewolf brought her a plate of eggs and bacon along with a pitcher of orange juice, and she sat out on the balcony to eat. She was only a block and a half from work, so she'd walk. She'd driven her personal car to Josef's, and her county car was in the lot, in case she needed it.

Josef's note had been cryptic. "I want the murdering bastard to suffer through deciding whether to confess or not, so he will confess in the next three days. The FBI is going to get him no matter when he confesses."

She'd asked him not to give her details, so she'd question Griffin blind. Now, she wanted to know more, but knew it was better this way. As agreed, she'd ripped the note into tiny pieces and flushed it.

Once in her office, Ronnie hit the ground running, continuing the search to find people who'd entered Griffin's life and mysteriously died or disappeared, and she found three more. A college girl he'd dated and broken up with, who three months later left Lee College on the way to her family in Townsend, and never arrived. He'd been questioned by the Cleveland police but had never been a suspect, since they'd broken up months earlier, and since he had an alibi — a new girlfriend who said he'd been with her the whole time.

He'd also gone on a missionary trip to South America with another church, and one of the women had gotten sick and died before they could get her into a town with a hospital. No reason to suspect him or anyone else. Cause of death was listed as dysentery. Had that been him? Ronnie didn't know, and there was no way to prove it.

On the same trip, a woman was found while being eaten by a black caiman, which was apparently a giant crocodile. No one knew whether the animal had killed her or had found her dead. The church had ceased all missionary trips after this one.

Towards the end of the day, she decided to take another crack at him. She really wanted to be the one to get the confession. Even if she had to hand him over to Graham, she wanted the confession first.

Ronnie needed to put this to bed for *all* the women he'd killed. They mattered, dammit.

Griffin was sitting in a chair, chained to the table, when she walked in. He looked haunted. His attorney was beside him, and she acknowledged him with a nod, but didn't speak to him.

"I'm Lieutenant Woods, you're Micah Griffin, accompanied by your attorney…"

She looked to the attorney, who filled in the name. "Jim Barabas."

She'd seen him plenty, but didn't remember his name.

She met Griffin's gaze again. "You've been read your rights, and I'm sure your attorney has coached you in them as well, yes?"

He nodded without looking at her.

"I need a verbal answer, sir."

"Yes. I know my rights, which apparently don't include the right to stay out of this damned box."

"Answer all my questions and there's a decent chance you won't have to come back." Well, back to *this* one, anyway.

Ronnie settled a picture of the woman who'd been eaten by a crocodile on the table. Then of the woman who'd died of dysentery. Then the woman who'd drowned in Cancun. She arranged pictures of five of the missing women in front of him. "Women who leave the country with you have a bad habit of not returning."

One hadn't left the country with him. Would he correct her?

When he'd silently stared at the women's images long enough she felt certain he wasn't going to comment, she said, "You find women in different states and counties, so law enforcement won't pick up on how often you show up in an investigation. Just asking questions of someone we don't think did it doesn't get you into a national database."

She touched the pictures and noted, "Bradley County Tennessee, Walker County Georgia, Catoosa County Georgia, and Hamilton County. It won't be hard to prove a pattern, now that we have it. I found these in twenty-four hours. How many more am I going to find, Mick?"

"You're fishing," said his attorney. "Ask him about the crimes he's been charged for, but this isn't—"

"We're building a case, Mr. Barabas, and your client needs to understand just how much hot water he's in. Are you aware you're representing a serial killer?"

"That's ludicrous. His girlfriend was murdered. He feels responsible because he didn't check on her as soon as she went missing. He confessed not because he killed her, but because he feels guilty."

Ronnie rolled her eyes. "Nice try counsellor, but no dice." She looked back to Griffin. "I wondered, last night before I dropped off to sleep, why you put Wendy in the zombie diorama. Did you decide she was evil, after all? Did she deserve to be displayed as evil? Did the bullet not cleanse her of her sins, as stoning would have?"

"She went there, without telling me. I looked through her phone and saw pictures of her with her friends, earlier in the week. She was a harlot."

Ronnie actually felt a little sorry for the attorney, who tried to talk over his client and get him to be quiet, but Griffin was determined to make Ronnie understand how Wendy deserved what she got.

"I see." She leaned back, looked at the stylus in her hand. "No, actually, I don't. If I'd killed all these women, I don't think I could sleep." She met his gaze. "I think I'd have nightmares. My guilty conscience would eat me from the inside out. The only way to cleanse your guilt is to confess, isn't it? God's everywhere, Mr. Griffin. He sees everything, *knows* everything."

Griffin stared at his hands as if he could see the blood on them, and whispered, "No."

Fifteen seconds later, he looked up. "I'd like my attorney to leave, please. Can you ask him to do that?"

The attorney threw his hands up, stood, gathered his tablet, and left. Ronnie figured someone would set him up down the hall so he could watch the proceedings. Everyone was being careful to cross every T and dot every I.

"He's gone, Mr. Griffin."

"I don't know all their names. I don't even know how I got to seventeen. How can so many women be so sinful?" He sighed. "And the one who most deserved to die is still alive."

Carter and Henderson had interviewed the ex-wife, found out he'd accused her of having sex with her boss because they'd had dinner at work while they finished a project. He'd beaten her up when she got home, and she'd filed for divorce. She'd dropped the request for a restraining order because the attorneys had negotiated — he'd give her the house and a fast divorce along with standard child support and visitation if she dropped her request for a restraining order and didn't press charges. She did, and the divorce happened fast. A restraining order would've meant more problems at work, and he was already in anger management classes for what his supervisor termed an explosive temper.

Six months later, he slapped her in front of the kids during pick-up for his visitation, and he agreed to supervised visitation if she wouldn't press charges. He stopped even trying to see his kids a few months later, and had been out of their lives ever since.

Sergeant Perry had found out Griffin had been moved into the passport office because he mostly worked alone in there, and thus didn't have to get along with his coworkers. Everyone tiptoed around him, but it's hard to fire someone from federal employment once they've made it through the first couple of years.

Ronnie decided not to bring the ex-wife into it — the danger was too great he'd go off track and not come back. He'd known he'd be the first person questioned if his ex-wife went missing or turned up dead. He might be a murdering asshole, but he was smart about how to do it without getting caught.

"Seventeen women? Who do you want to tell me about first?"

"She's buried under the patio at 5327 Stuart Street, in Ringgold. I buried her that night, and went and bought the paver stones, gravel, sand, and concrete the next morning. She's under the back patio. She was my first. A whore. Whores don't deserve to live."

Georgia. Josef had been right. Graham was getting him. She'd already known he would, but this cemented it. Didn't matter anymore — she needed to get as much of his confession as she could.

Chapter Twenty

Josef listened to Griffin's confession through Corey's mind, since he was managing what they called the viewing room, and was the person speaking into Lieutenant Woods' ear piece.

She must've started shortly before he awakened, and he'd moved things along a few times — made Griffin see blood on his hands once, and gave him brief flashes of his nightmares a couple of times.

Ronnie had food brought in at seven that evening, and she finally left the tiny little room a little after ten. When they were finished, she had a spoken confession of all seventeen murders, and then the bastard had signed seventeen sheets of paper, admitting to the murder of each woman.

Josef waited until she left the room to try to telepath her.

Can you hear me.

Yes.

Let me come pick you up? You need sleep.

Give me a few minutes and I'll call you on my phone.

He stayed in Corey's head, saw her step into the viewing room, saw her team give her high fives. Perry, their resident seasoned detective, looked at her appraisingly, as if making sure she was okay. For that matter, they all did, each in their own way — the ex-marine, the psych major, even the geek. Her team was concerned.

It isn't often one encounters evil, and she'd needed to be friendly and nice to the murdering son of a bitch to get the entire confession. It was no wonder so many detectives drank. You can't just shake that kind of thing off.

"I'm fine," she told her men. "I need to get my phone from my office and make a personal call. Graham's going to get this one, too, but I'm okay with that. Micah Griffin will die in jail."

"This is why you get the big bucks," Henderson joked. She rolled her eyes at him, but then Corey turned back to the computer and Josef could only hear them.

"The commander watched for nearly an hour," Myers told her. "We had lots of other visitors, too. You sure you're okay? I'm not sure *I* am, and I didn't have to play nice with the motherfucker."

"I need to bleach my brain, but yeah. I'll be okay. I'm headed to my office, if anyone needs me, catch me in the next ten minutes because I'm about to leave."

"You want to go somewhere for drinks?" Myers asked.

"Not tonight."

She walked out, and Josef stayed put in Corey's head. He wanted to know what they said after she left.

"If it was anyone else, I don't think I'd let them walk out of the building alone," said Sergeant Perry.

"I still don't really want her to," said Myers, "but I doubt we can stop her."

"I'd contact the Commander if I thought she wasn't handling it," Carter said, leaned against a wall. "She's fine, but I have no idea how. I wasn't in that room, and I'm with you — I'll be okay, but I'm not right now. I'll go down the street for that drink, if you want."

"No one can be expected to be okay after hearing that," said Perry. "We'll process it and put it behind us, same as always. It's what we do. I'll have a drink with ya'll, too."

Josef's phone rang, and he pulled out of Corey's head. "*Bellula.*"

"Do you want to come in and meet my team, or do you just want to pick me up in the parking lot?"

"They're worried about you. I should come in and ease their minds."

"Okay. I'll tell the front desk to send you up."

167

Ronnie let her hair down and pulled a jacket from her wardrobe. She grabbed a chocolate bar from her desk, and sat and ate it, eyes closed. Two minutes of dark silence while eating chocolate gave her the strength to step back into her murder room. Carter and Myers were in there, sitting at their desks, typing — no doubt catching up on things they'd missed while watching her with Griffin.

The elevator dinged and everyone looked up. A uniformed deputy walked Josef into the room, both of them loaded down with boxes of food. Her mouth watered and her stomach growled.

"I brought Buffalo wings, cheese sticks, fried mushrooms, and a couple of pizzas with every kind of meat except anchovies. I assume you're hungry, and figured your team would be, too."

Ronnie smiled. He knew how to get cops to like him — feed them.

"Call everyone," she told Myers.

The uniformed deputy looked at her, unsure, and she motioned to the boxes. "Take two plates with you, so whoever's on the front desk gets some, too."

She'd seen the stack of plates he'd brought. There was more than enough.

Josef put everything down and walked to her. "You look tired, Lieutenant."

"Long day. Josef Romano, Deputy Gabriel Myers and Detective Jamison Carter. Myers, Carter, this is Josef, my… crap. I guess he's my boyfriend."

Both of her men looked dumbfounded.

Myers recovered first, and stepped forward to shake his hand. "It's nice to meet you, Josef. You know this is kind of like meeting *all* of the big brothers, yes?"

"I gathered. She thinks the world of her team, It's nice to finally meet you."

"Finally? How long has she kept you under wraps?"

"Long enough," Ronnie told them. The elevator dinged and the rest of her team arrived.

Ronnie made herself a plate and let the men do their thing, her exhaustion of earlier not so bad while she watched them gradually accept Josef.

After four plates of food, she stood and walked to him. Her men had grilled the vampire, and he'd graciously held his own. They were discussing college football now, and it was time for her to find a bed.

"Ya'll polish off the food and clean up," she told her team. "Josef and I are out of here. If we don't get called out on a new case, I plan to sleep in. I'll see ya'll at ten."

Chapter Twenty-One

Four days later, and Ronnie had been watching the clock all damned day. She'd told her Captain she needed to leave at four. She was never sick, never needed to go to the dentist, and didn't even bother having her hair cut by a stylist because it just went back to long and wavy when she *changed* back from the tiger.

So, leaving an hour early shouldn't have been a problem, except for the fact it seemed to come out of left field.

"Are you okay?" he'd asked.

"I'm fine. Barring an all-out gang war or the murder of a prominent citizen, I'm hoping ya'll can give me an uninterrupted evening."

He sat back with a knowing smile. "Other than scheduled vacation days, I can't remember you ever asking for a personal day, a sick day, time to go to the doctor or dentist…" He shrugged. "You want the evening free to shag your new man, you have it. You come in early and leave late all the time. I'm not worried about a measly hour."

"Shag? Seriously? How does that even work? I mean, *screw* at least makes sense. Shag is just ugly carpet."

She'd left his office, secure in the knowledge they'd leave her alone unless something truly awful happened.

Some women might be offended at the *shag* comment, but Ronnie understood he'd treated her exactly as he would've spoken to a male Lieutenant, and she appreciated the fact her department didn't feel the need to treat her with kid gloves.

The night Josef had come to her office, after she'd been locked in the box with Griffin for so damned long, Josef had massaged her until she was one big limp noodle, and then fucked her unconscious. She'd offered her neck to him, but he'd told her he wouldn't drink from her for the first time after such an emotional evening.

And now it was four days later, and he still hadn't drank from her, despite her telling him she was ready. Every day, he'd already fed by the time she got to his house.

Today, she'd arrive before he awakened.

Josef rose at nearly four thirty and leapt to his feet. The light over his door was orange, which meant there was a security issue. Green meant everything was as it should be, yellow meant something was amiss with no specific threat, and red meant the coterie was under attack. Orange meant the threat was real but an attack wasn't underway.

He telepathed the daytime security chief — a trusted werewolf.

Sitrep. Now.

Sir. Lieutenant Woods arrived at four-twenty and demanded we take her to you. We told her we had no orders to do so, and we'd check with you upon rising. I'm afraid... He sighed. *We knew you wouldn't want her harmed, but our first priority is your safety while the sun has you in its grip.*

Josef could see what had happened in the man's memories, and he suppressed a grin. All three wolves at this location had stood in front of the door, so she'd have needed to physically move them in order to get to him. They'd telepathed to the wolves at the coterie house, and now five wolves stood between him and the Lieutenant.

Thank you for managing the situation without having to handle her. Hold your pattern another couple of minutes I'll let you know when to stand down.

He reached out with his mind and found hers.

If I'd known you'd arrive before I awakened, I'd have altered instructions for my security team. They're under orders to subdue and detain anyone who attempts contact with me while I'm unconscious, but wisely decided upon another course of action with you.

I wanted to surprise you. They ruined the surprise.

173

He chuckled, and let her feel it through the mental connection. *I'll change their instructions so you're allowed downstairs, but my security at this time doesn't allow anyone into my room. I must open the final door from inside.*

He connected with the wolf again. *Please bring her to me.*

As you wish, Sir.

Ronnie was mastering the art of shielding, so he had no idea why she'd come so early. He'd undressed before lying down to let the sun take him, and he only had time to put a robe on before he needed to open the door and let her in.

"Is everything okay?" She smelled aggravated, but that likely had more to do with his security team thwarting her than anything else.

"I wanted to get here before you'd fed, so you couldn't keep putting me off."

Josef crossed his arms, remembered that's a no-no in modern society, but decided he didn't give a rat's ass.

"You aren't ready to feed me yet."

"You don't know what I'm ready for! Is there something wrong with my blood? Why don't you…" She crossed her arms and turned away from him.

"You're right — I don't know what's in your head. So long as you keep your shields up to keep me from seeing your reasons for wanting to feed me, I'll continue to believe you aren't ready." He sighed. "You're too important to me,

Bellula. I won't risk screwing everything up by feeding from you when you truly aren't ready for it yet."

She took a breath, let it out, and dropped her shields. She still faced away from him, but she let him see everything — the confusion around the time she'd been bitten before was still there, but it wasn't the problem he'd assumed it would be. Her reasons all had to do with the present, with wanting to feed and nourish him, but even more so, wanting him to smell like her. Ronnie and her inner tiger seemed to be in agreement — they didn't like him smelling so much like his wolves, but smelling like a different cat was *completely* out of the question.

And because the cat wanted it, too, he knew exactly how the first bite had to happen.

Two steps and he was to her, vampire fast. He turned her to him and expected her to fight him, but she shifted towards him and let him bend her backwards and take her mouth. He could almost taste her already, but it wasn't time yet. She needed to be naked and under him. He needed to be inside her the first time he fully tasted his feisty little tiger.

Need slammed into him like a fist in the gut, and he ripped her shirt off, pushed her bra aside, and sucked at her nipple. More torture, because he wanted to bite in the *worst* sort of way — and he would, but not yet.

He lifted her, carried her to his bed, dropped her on it, and finished demolishing her clothes. His cop thought about protesting, but her arrow-sharp gaze softened, and she spread her legs. Inviting him.

Okay, so the cat could be dealt with later — the woman needed something different.

Josef let his robe fall from his shoulders and tossed it onto a nearby bench before climbing between her legs. He drove into her without warning. No more foreplay, no finesse — she wasn't going to relax until he'd fed from her, and he *needed* her blood.

She gasped at his unexpected invasion, and he closed his eyes because she was so damned tight around him. Tight, hot, wet, and delicious.

Delicious.

If he'd let his hunger dictate, the bite would've been hard and fast, but that wasn't how this first time needed to go, so he controlled his own urges, directed as much pain killer to his fangs as he could ahead of time, and then licked and kissed the side of her neck. With so much painkiller aimed at his fangs, his saliva would also have a large concentration.

Some humans and shapeshifters preferred to feel the fangs entering, but he didn't want to hurt his *Bellula*.

Chapter Twenty-Two

Ronnie wanted him to just bite her and get it over with already, and thought he was about to, but he licked her throat and pressed his palm over her clit, and she thought she'd *die* of need. Her pulse had been pounding in her ears, and now she felt it in her clit, her nipples. Heat surged through her veins, and her pussy clenched around his cock buried inside her.

She pushed at him impatiently, trying to incite him to move, to bite. Her hips rotated under him, unable to stay still.

"*Need.*"

She hadn't meant to say anything, but the single word had come out. Pleading.

One of his hands angled her head so the side of her neck was elongated, and the talented fingers of his other hand massaged all around her clit without touching it.

Before she could protest, his fangs were at her skin, and then oh-so-slowly sank in.

She felt the pressure of them pushing in, and imagined she felt the holes being created and then widened, but she didn't feel the sharp pain she expected. Before, the vampire had bit fast, sucked, and sucked, and sucked until she hadn't wanted him stop.

But Josef slid his fangs into her painlessly. His fangs *and* his cock were inside her.

The second the thought went through her head, he sucked, and it was as if a line went from her clit to his fangs. He pressed on her clit with his palm when he stopped sucking, and massaged around it again for the next long, intense pull of her blood into his mouth.

His cock pulsed inside her, which made her pussy muscles spasm around him. His hand and mouth worked in congress, so he massaged her clit while he sucked, and then pressed the area while he didn't — as if he could push more blood into her throat, which was ridiculous, but...

He stopped drinking. Goosebumps surfaced over her entire body when the fangs pulled out. A groan escaped her throat, and her desperation echoed through the room. His tongue laved the holes in her throat, and then he moved over her and finally gave her all of him. Ronnie spread her legs wider, planted her feet, and fucked him right back — hard and fast and perfect.

Her climax slammed through her without warning, and she screamed and writhed under him, but he didn't slow, and her release grew larger and larger, without an end in sight. Her insides jerked and moved until she wondered if anyone had ever died from too much pleasure, and then her mind was a blank because words were too much. Nothing existed except Josef inside her, taking her.

Josef kept her on top of the climax until he worried she might pass out, and only then did he slow his hips and let her catch her breath.

But not long, because he still needed to feed from the cat.

Not literally, of course, but he knew how to bring the cat's personality to the surface. How to make sure both the woman *and* the cat felt as if they'd fed him.

He flipped her over, put her knees under her, and flattened her body. Eventually, she'd learn this was called knees and chest, but words would push the tiger away. He drove into her again, hard and merciless, fucked her fast and brutal for thirty seconds, grabbed the back of her neck, and aimed his fangs for the side — the opposing side, so he wouldn't drink from the same spot twice in the same day. He stopped fucking her a half-second before he struck, and this time, he let her *feel* the bite.

He'd seen the need for this when she'd let her shields down. She needed him to stop treating her like a rape victim. She wanted it *all*, and he was giving it to her — but he was also closely monitoring her scent, her pulse, and her thoughts. She hadn't put the shield back up, and her thoughts were an open book.

He didn't drink much this time — a dozen strong pulls, but she was coming again before he'd finished the first because he injected an orgasm cocktail designed to shoot her straight to bliss.

He made Ronnie *change* to her tiger when they finished, but she didn't stay in her cat form more than three or four minutes before she *changed* back. She had too much to say. Luckily, the cat was in agreement and didn't argue.

"Unless it's an emergency, or you need to make a political statement, I'm the only cat you feed from."

He chuckled. "Your tiger is spectacular, *Bellula*. I hope you'll let me spend more time with her later."

"No other cats," she repeated.

"I can give you that."

"I'm not sore anymore. *Dammit*."

Josef couldn't resist his chuckle. "You wanted me to smell like you, and I only took so much because I knew you could replenish by *changing*. If you wish to be sore, I'll be more than happy to comply once you've eaten."

Chapter Twenty-Three

Seven months later

Lieutenant Veronica Woods sat at the back of a federal courthouse, despite the fact she didn't need to be present. She'd testified a few days before; today was just the sentencing. She was usually okay with finding out after the fact, but she needed to see and hear the conclusion. She needed to see Griffin led away, needed to see the look in his eyes when he heard that he would never again be a free man.

She wasn't terribly surprised when Agent Graham sat beside her. He'd had to hand the case off to a serial killer unit, but he was emotionally invested in it, too.

"Where's your team?" Graham asked.

"Where's yours?"

He shrugged. "Working on leads for other cases, which is where I should be, but I needed to see this."

"Same answer."

"Yeah."

Ramirez and Flores had already been sentenced. Ramirez had received eighteen months for his part in the bribery scheme, though Ronnie expected he'd be released close to the six month mark if he kept his nose clean, since the judge was clear he was eligible for parole. Flores, however, was going to be in a cage until he was an old man, because the judge had been just as clear that he would *not* be eligible for parole for at least forty years. Flores received eight years for attempting to bribe a federal employee, with another six years added on because the bribe included drug trafficking. He got another twenty years for rape, and then twelve more years for threatening gang rape if she didn't stop talking to law enforcement. Threatening further *great bodily harm* during the commission of an assault carries a longer sentence then merely offering money as a bribe. With the addition of a few smaller offenses, Flores' total sentence ended up being a few months shy of fifty-eight years. He was twenty-four at sentencing, and he'd be inside until he was at *least* sixty-four years old.

"Tigre's the only one we couldn't make charges stick to. The old man should call himself Teflon." He'd been arrested more times than she'd wanted to count, and had never plea bargained or been found guilty.

"You didn't show up for Flores' sentencing," he noted.

She shrugged. "Flores is most certainly a criminal who deserves every year the judge gave him, but he isn't…" She looked away, unwilling to let Graham see whatever emotions she might let slip out. "I rarely use the word evil, but Griffin…" She shuddered.

"You recognized while he was confessing that his actions didn't follow that of most serial killers," Graham noted. "Only a few of his victims were killed in the same manner. He didn't have a set procedure. Every murder was different — drowning, strangulation, fed to a crocodile while still alive, gunshot wound to different body parts, a knife to the heart—"

"Right," Ronnie interrupted, "so while most serial killers are forever chasing the thrill of the first kill, some of his later kills were actually a bigger thrill than his first. However, he didn't see it as a thrill, but as his way of avenging God and punishing sinners, which…"

The room went silent when the courthouse doors were closed, and Ronnie took a deep, cleansing breath. She'd discovered and then been assigned number seventeen, and there wouldn't be an eighteen. He would never kill another innocent woman, because she'd fucking *stopped* him.

The judge talked about how a court proceeding with a signed confession was usually merely a formality, but that they'd needed time to document each murder — even those that happened in other countries, because the women lived here. Met him here. Expected to return here.

He thanked everyone for their patience, and then turned his attention to Griffin.

"Sir, you had a good job, a good wife, a nice house. When you assaulted your wife, you'd already been to anger management classes twice. You knew you had a problem, but you chose not to deal with it.

"Your decisions to murder were precise, calculated. The choices you made are despicable. You're of above average intelligence, and you clearly worked through how to stay off of law enforcement's radar."

The judge shook his head. "This case has once again brought to light the challenge of the people society have forgotten. Those without family, without friends who'll check on them. That you met six of them at various churches, where lonely people tried to connect with others, is especially heinous."

The judge talked another five minutes before he mentioned Ronnie, and she felt eyes turning to look at her, because the judge's gaze practically bored through her. "Lieutenant Woods, I have no idea how you managed to hold it together for the marathon confession, but you are made of some mighty strong stuff. For every person who makes me fear for our future, I find ten people who show me we're going to be okay, and you, Lieutenant Woods, are one of those people. Thank you for fighting for the victims, even when no one else cares about them. Thank you for giving me hope for our future."

Ronnie tipped her head down and back up. Speaking wasn't appropriate, so it was all she knew to do.

The judge talked another ten minutes, detailing Griffin's crimes and naming every victim except for the one they could never put a name to. Many of them had family after all, and the families were there, finally getting closure.

And then, finally, the part Ronnie had waited for — the death penalty, which absolutely didn't mean he'd be killed, because the federal government hadn't executed anyone since 2003, but it meant Griffin would never see more than an hour of daylight per day for the rest of his godforsaken life.

Ronnie bought more than a few rounds of drinks that evening — not that Josef would actually let her pay for them, but she'd have bought them even if it'd been out of her paycheck.

She wasn't usually terribly extravagant, but she needed to show her team how much they meant to her. How much she appreciated them.

When her overprotective vampire had learned her team frequented the bar in this particular historic building, he'd bought the building and the bar. She'd wanted to throttle him for it, at first — she was more than capable of taking care of herself.

However, she'd eventually had to admit it was nice to be able to cut up and let loose without having to watch her back. The bouncers, bartender, and waitstaff were all werewolves or cats, and they all knew they were to protect Ronnie and "her cops" above all else. Ronnie had argued with him the civilians needed protecting, but Josef was adamant she'd have a safe place to let loose and chill out with her people.

Tonight, she polished off her second burger at close to ten o'clock, stood, and said her goodbyes. Despite the fact she told them she'd be okay, Myers still walked her to her car.

"Josef is due back tonight, right?"

"Yeah. Sorry to cut the celebration short, but I've missed him."

"He's good for you. Enjoy the rest of your evening."

Her team had welcomed Josef into the fold, but he'd known how to win them over. Anytime they worked late, he showed up with food. He'd learned everyone's favorite, and he made sure he brought a spread that made them all happy. He'd also shown up — more times than she could count — with enough mugs of hot coffee for them all when he knew they had to be out in the cold at night. When he took care of her, he also took care of her people.

He'd been gone for ten days though, and she'd missed him something terrible. He'd accompanied Abbott on a trip to deal with an out-of-control wolf alpha in another territory. She'd had to be okay knowing Josef would be feeding and fucking from various shapeshifters in a show of power — a way to establish the hierarchy.

They weren't in Abbott's territory, but the Master Vampire of that territory hadn't been able to gain control of the town, so the Concilio had asked him to do so. Josef said it never hurts to earn favor with them, so they went.

Honestly, she was fine with him fucking someone for political reasons, as a show of power, but she'd told him if she ever found out he fucked anyone romantically besides her, she'd rip his balls off, watch them grow back, and rip them off again.

She'd meant it, and he'd believed her.

However, as their relationship had progressed, she'd realized the threat wasn't necessary. He'd be true to his word because it was the kind of person he was.

Her vampire fed from her a few times a week when he was in town, and from other non-feline shapeshifters the rest of the time — but he didn't screw them. Not anymore.

Ronnie slid out of the too-fancy SUV Josef had surprised her with on her birthday, and stepped into the hangar's office area. The manager recognized her and motioned towards a monitor. "They aren't far. Maybe ten minutes."

Ronnie closed her eyes and pushed her consciousness towards him. Now that he'd had her blood, he could talk to her from a much farther distance, and it was also easier for her to initiate contact.

His voice came into her head, and it was like music for her soul.

I've missed you, Bellula. It'll be good to get home.

I might've noticed you were gone a few times, she teased. *Can we go straight home, or do you have other responsibilities to get to, first?*

Straight home. Everything else can wait until you're asleep.

187

Dating a vampire wasn't as complicated as she'd first assumed. He slept while she worked. He awoke and handled some of his obligations from his basement, until she arrived home, and then she had his undivided attention, most nights. Once she went to sleep, usually a little before midnight, he had the rest of the night for his security obligations. They had their evenings together, and they both had their jobs.

She waited for him to come to her, when he got off the plane, and she gladly went into his arms when he neared her and opened them, inviting her into his embrace. She closed her eyes and leaned into him, happy to feel his energy. His scent was off because he hadn't fed from her in so long, but he still smelled like Josef. God, how she'd missed him. Her heart settled into her chest a little easier.

He hadn't fed yet, but he wasn't overly hungry. He'd have taken a few sips from one of the wolves on the plane if he'd needed it.

"A life on death row, knowing they probably won't kill him, but might…" Josef held her a little tighter. "It's as much as you could hope for within the current societal constraints."

Josef was a firm believer in the death penalty, and thought a swift, public, and gruesome execution was the best way to prevent more crime.

"I know. It's behind me, now. The case is closed. There won't even be parole hearings to deal with." She shrugged. "I bought several rounds of drinks tonight. It's behind us. You had a successful trip?"

He took her keys from her hand and tossed them to a werewolf who stood ten feet away with Josef's luggage. "Come. We'll talk while I drive us home. You have entirely too many clothes on for my liking."

She'd worn a suit to court, and still had on the skirt and blouse. Spring had hit in the south, so she wasn't actually wearing that many clothes.

Josef eyed the luggage in the back of the SUV to be sure everything was there, retrieved Ronnie's keys from the wolf, and walked her to the passenger side to put her in. He always drove when it was the two of them.

When they were on their way, he answered her earlier question. "We deposed the Alpha Wolf, removed those who would've continued his regime, and made sure we left people in place who would fix his many, many wrongs. Abbott moved another Strigorii master in to run the city, and we found appropriate situations for the slaves. As always, some will eventually be rehabilitated, while the others will likely need someone to watch out for them the rest of their lives."

"Sometimes, I'm envious of those who police the supernaturals, because you can walk in and *fix* the situation without having to deal with so much red tape, and without having to risk a judge fucking everything up." She blew out a breath. "But I'll keep my job policing humans. I'm not sure I could…" Ronnie shook her head. She was glad the judge stepped in and handled the actual consequences. Her job was to the find the bad guys and hand them off to the justice system.

"On the contrary, you know you could, you just worry you'd enjoy it too much. If you could've killed Griffin after he confessed, things would be so much simpler."

"Maybe." She changed the subject. "Your energy is smoother this time."

He'd come home from one of these trips full of the blood of human traffickers. She could *smell* the evil, and she'd made him drink from her until his energy was right again.

Chapter Twenty-Four

Josef hadn't expected her to sense the difference, that first time he'd helped Abbott clean out a city. She was a cop, and it seemed she could sniff out a criminal.

And she'd hated it when he'd smelled like one.

So, he merely took sips from the bad guys now, enough to get fully into their heads and see their crimes, and no more. He drank his fill from people not involved, or from shapeshifters they'd brought with them.

"Anything I need to know about the people you fucked?" she asked.

This was their deal — full disclosure because she wanted to know. The cop in her *needed* to know.

"Seven male vampires and two female. Three male wolves and one female. I made the wolves show me their belly and spread their legs to start — full submission. I fed from and fucked one of the men every day, and took him from behind after the first day, usually bent over something, or leaned against a wall. Also, I fucked two male cheetahs, but only took in enough of their blood to get fully into their heads." He sighed. "We had to kill *all* of the bears. It was a bad situation — a commune in the middle of nowhere in Montana. I fucked one bear in the hopes…" He shook his head. "They'd been the leaders, and I hoped the younger bears might be salvageable, but we had to kill every last one of them. It was nothing more than a camp to grow soldiers for the dark side — shapeshifters of every type, drawn there because of what they were allowed to do to the human slaves. We killed all leaders and over half of the soldiers. They'd taken over an existing town, and every human was enslaved."

Which explained why the actual supernatural police force — the Concilio — hadn't stepped in for so long. As long as there was no chance *free* humans might find out about supernaturals, they wouldn't get involved.

"Why were you called in?"

"I can't talk much about it. Concilio secrets." He reached for her hand and lifted it to his lips to give it a quick kiss. "It's good to be home. Abbott's territory runs like clockwork, with vampires and humans living in harmony — the vampires in the shadows and the humans everywhere, sunlight *and* shadows, as it should be."

"And yet, you enjoy the occasional trip where you get to unleash your sadistic tendencies."

"Usually, but not this one." He'd had to explain how he sometimes enjoyed hurting people while he fed from them, and then it'd taken him weeks to convince his *Bellula* he never wanted to hurt her — he wanted to taste joy and bliss from her. Never pain. *Never.*

If she enjoyed pain, it would be different, but it wasn't in her to enjoy it. She'd moved past her many childhood rapes by always being in control during sex, and while she gladly let him take control and give her orgasms, she'd never be able to enjoy him hurting her.

Josef had worried about her getting a rape case, and how she'd handle it. She worked Major Crimes, and was specifically given the high profile cases. So, he'd gone through the minds of the Commander and Majors, and anyone else involved in the decision of which detectives get which cases, intending to make it so they'd never knowingly give her a sex crime, but it turned out, they were already being careful not to. This didn't mean she wouldn't occasionally end up with one, because it wasn't always something they knew up front, but the entire chain of command went out of their way to take care of her. They knew her strengths and her weaknesses, and they played to her strengths.

Josef pulled his love's vehicle into their driveway and parked by the back door. He wanted her too badly to bother with the garage tonight.

"Inside, Lieutenant. I need you. It's been too long."

Nine days without her had been torture. His soul *ached* without her energy to balance him.

Nathan told him she'd gone to the Pride's property Friday after work and had stayed a tiger until Sunday evening. She hadn't been called to a crime all weekend, and she'd been the tiger all weekend. She'd missed him, too.

Ronnie started unbuttoning her blouse on the walk to the back door. Her vampire had a tendency to rip her clothes off and buy her more, and she had too many already because Josef loved buying her clothes as much as he enjoyed feeding her.

She'd moved in with him a month to the day after they met, and had never regretted it, even for a moment. Josef was her soul mate. Her heart ached with the loss of him when he was away too long.

They both discarded clothing on the way to the upstairs fake master suite. Their actual bedroom was downstairs, but neither was in the mood to get through all of those security doors.

Ronnie ripped her own panties off as she stepped into the room, her impatience too much. "Hard and fast the first time. *Please* don't try to be sweet!"

"As you wish."

She let him tumble her over the bed, the shock of it vibrating through her. His impatient hands held her, his feet spread her legs, and he entered her fast and hard, just as she'd asked. His thick cock stretched her wide, and a groan escaped her chest.

"Yeeeesssss." Her voice was half pleading and half satisfied. She had him, finally, but she needed more.

He moved inside her, wild, reckless. Waves of pleasure flowed through her, but she needed to be inside him, too.

"*Josef.*"

It was a request, and as close as she ever got to begging, but he'd never make her do that.

Sometimes, he bit slow and she barely felt it, but today, he struck like a snake, and it was perfect. She wanted to be inside him. Wanted to nourish him. Feed him.

He smelled wrong without her blood in his veins. He was *hers*. He was supposed to smell like her.

His lips sealed around the bite. Every suck pulled at her clit as well as the side of her neck. He didn't fuck her while he drank, but his cock pulsed with her blood. Her heat. Her lifeforce.

He took a lot, but she was a shapeshifter and she'd make more. When he finally withdrew his fangs, his cock pulled out, slammed home. Stopped. He licked the bite and she shuddered.

"Stop playing and *fuck* me, dammit."

"So bossy."

She was just about to flip them over so she could ride him, and he finally gave her what she wanted — rapid fire, faster than humanly-possible fucking. Hard, fast, and in just the right spot inside her.

Ronnie's legs went limp, her arms no longer held her in place, and an orgasm swept over her like a tidal wave, inundating her with pleasure and bliss until she didn't think she could take anymore, but she knew she could — and would.

Josef drank from her three more times and gave her countless orgasms before she fell asleep, worn out as only her vampire could make her. Nothing mattered when she was in his arms. Even the dead left her alone.

Epilogue

Halloween fell on a Sunday this year, which should've meant Detective Veronica Woods had a day off before the festivities, but her city was in the middle of a gang war, and her team worked with the gang task force on the most publicized crimes. However, she sent everyone home at four o'clock. There wasn't much more they could do until morning, anyway.

Abbott was throwing a huge Halloween bash at the Hamilton Place location of The Billiard Club. A private party, invitation only. Ronnie always did something with her girls on Halloween, and Josef had encouraged her to invite them.

Her vampire had also invited her team from work. This meant the people from three different parts of her lives would be there, but she was surprisingly calm about it.

The couple had stayed in Josef's room at the coterie house the night before, and now, the vampires and their partners were downstairs getting ready. Even Abbott and Spence, who'd be going as Batman and Robin.

Fawne helped spray red and blue onto Ronnie's two ponytails, and then took her seat again at the long mirror. Ronnie and Josef were going as Harley Quinn and the Joker, Kendra was going as the new version of Wonder Woman, in a sexy black metallic-looking bodysuit, while Eric would be Superman.

And Fawne kicked ass as Enchantress.

The women did their own makeup, but offered pointers about eyeliner and contouring until all three looked perfect.

They slid into their costumes and walked into the downstairs living room together, arm-in-arm, laughing.

Ronnie's heart skipped a few beats at Josef in his black pants and purple jacket, his hair slicked back, black eyeliner with charcoal shading around his eyes, and deep red lip dye. The silly mouth wasn't drawn on, and Josef *rocked* the look.

He'd fed from her and given her uncountable orgasms an hour before, and she wanted him again, but they'd mess their make-up all to hell and back if they... she almost didn't care, but tonight was about their friends — his people and her people in the same room. Isn't that what couples do? Merge groups of friends?

A side door opened, and Ronnie's stomach turned over when Gavin and Queenie walked through. She didn't much like Gavin, but avoiding him was impossible. Josef merely told her to trust her instincts, but assured her she was safe around him.

Gavin was supposed to be the Green Arrow, but he'd decided to be the street clothes version and not the costumed one, so he was wearing black leather pants and a black silk shirt, which was pretty much what he always wore. Queenie, however, was the Black Canary, with black leather short-shorts and bustier, and a cute little black leather bolero shrug — and sky high heels, which was Queenie's trademark. Ronnie had never seen her in anything less than four-inch heels, and tonight's were even higher, but Queenie seemed perfectly natural in them.

Ronnie knew the instant the sun dipped below the horizon, because the vampires grew stronger. She rubbed her arms to smooth the goose bumps — she only got them when she was with a group of vampires, because the air always seemed electrified when they came into power. Most vampires didn't awaken until the sun went down, but these were the uber-powerful, so they rose earlier.

Abbott stood, the perfect Batman to Spence's Robin. "That's our cue to leave. Gavin and Queenie are driving alone, but Spence and I are in the limo if anyone wants to ride with us. We'll return to the mountain tonight, but we can swing by here to drop people off, first."

Kendra, Eric, and Fawne rode with him, but Josef turned down the offer since they were acting as designated driver for some of Ronnie's friends.

They picked three of her four friends up, one after another — Silk, Gamora, and Jessica Jones. Amy and her new husband were coming as Ant-man and Wasp, and were driving themselves.

Josef was protective over Ronnie's friends, which was yet another reason she'd fallen head-over-heels in love with him. The spark at the beginning had been important, but she genuinely *liked* being around him. They fit, the ancient general and the modern-day major crimes lieutenant.

Josef let everyone out under the portico before he parked the car, and Isaac gave Ronnie a hug when he saw her. She introduced him to her friends, and noted, "You're Mr. Incredible, right?" At his nod, she added, "I can't wait to see the rest of your little family."

He chuckled. "Francisco had to be Elastiman to pull it off, but Cassie is Violet and Cam is Dash, so it worked."

"Does this mean Mr. Incredible is taken?" Mandy asked as they stepped away from him.

"Sorry, but he has two boyfriends and a girlfriend, so yeah."

Before getting involved with Josef, Ronnie hadn't hugged anyone except her closest girlfriends, and she'd been intimidating enough that no one else tried. Well, except for Nathan, but no one intimidates him.

However, Josef's friends were huggers, and not easily intimidated, so she'd had to get used to it. On this night, she hugged them and was happy to do it. His friends had become her friends, and her friends had become his.

She still didn't hug her coworkers, but that was different.

Speaking of her team, she saw Myers first, dressed as The Incredible Hulk, complete with bulging muscles that weren't fake. His girlfriend was Betty Ross, in a red unitard with a fancy black buttoned leotard over it. Ronnie hugged his girlfriend and welcomed her. She'd met her at the bar a few times — it might be time to research the girl and see if she was worthy of dating her best deputy. Speaking of which, she looked at Myers. "You ready for the exam next week?"

"I am, LT. I'll do you proud."

He was taking the detective's exam, and if he failed it she'd give him shit jobs until he passed it — and she'd told him as much. Many times.

He was going to pass it, though. Myers didn't do anything halfway.

"Of course he is. He's had you teaching him."

Ronnie turned at Sergeant Perry's gruff voice, and frowned. He was in his usual tweed pants and dress shirt. "Who are you dressed as?"

"Myself. I'm a goddamned superhero. Didn't you know?"

"Of course you are," Josef said as he stepped to them. "We'll call you Grumpy Man, able to tell when someone's lying with a single frown."

Perry glowered at him, but his eyes were happy, and that didn't happen often. "Every group has a smart ass. The Joker fits you."

Carter and Henderson walked up together — Henderson an absolutely stunning Black Panther, while Carter was in jeans and a supertight black t-shirt that showed every muscle. And Carter has a *lot* of muscles.

"*Two* of my team didn't dress up? Really?" Ronnie said with a laugh. "Ya'll are a disappointment!"

"What?" said Carter, indignant. "I'm Luke Cage!"

Ronnie shook her head at him, and then turned at RaeLynn's voice. "Nathan pulled the same stunt. He's dressed as he always is, but with a shiny yellow glove on one hand. He says he's Iron Fist." She waved at her navy blue unitard with the pale yellow sewn into the right places up top, and said, "I'm Kitty Pryde. Seemed fitting."

"It's perfect," Ronnie said, hugging her friend. Nathan had taken Ronnie to RaeLynn's grandmother the morning after that horrible night, so RaeLynn felt a little like a cousin.

Ronnie played pool and drank beer with her team. She did shots and danced with her girlfriends. She drank margaritas with the women from the coterie house, and she took Josef downstairs to make him take a few sips of her while she was tipsy. She didn't often drink enough to feel it, and she knew it wouldn't last long, but she *needed* to share it with him.

If someone had told her a year earlier that she'd be downstairs with the aloof vampire, taking her Harley Quinn sequined panties off in a downstairs office of TBC and demanding a quickie feed-and-fuck, she'd have thought them delusional.

And yet, here she was, doing just that while she unzipped his pants and pulled him out.

"What time is it?" she asked. "About the time we first saw each other, right? We'll call it an anniversary fuck."

"Oh, I have plans after the party to celebrate our one year anniversary, and there will be *nothing* quick about them, but for now…" He lifted her, pressed her against the wall, and drove into her. "I believe I can accommodate your request. The office is soundproof, feel free to scream in three, two…"

He scraped across *the spot* inside her, jackhammer fast, and she was just tipsy enough that within seconds she was swept away in bliss.

Josef walked to the back wall and looked in the mirror behind the huge plant. He was amazed the lip dye hadn't smeared. The same couldn't be said of his little tiger's lipstick.

She put her sequined panties back on, adjusted the belt over them, and pulled a tube of lipstick from her bra. She glanced in the mirror, saw the lipstick all around her mouth, and sighed.

"This is a vampire's office. Where are the baby wipes?"

He chuckled and retrieved them. "Not a vampire's office, but close enough."

She casually repaired the bottom part of her face — so matter of fact on the outside, but he knew she wanted him again already. That was okay, he wanted her again, too. They'd stay until the end, take her friends home, and the wait would make the rest of their evening even sweeter.

"Nathan made a short appearance and didn't stay long. He and Abbott in the same room is still…" She sighed, and Josef agreed with the sentiment.

The Abbott and Amakhosi had a treaty in place once again, but there was zero trust between them.

"He let RaeLynn stay," Josef pointed out. "Things are better. Speaking of which, did you notice Mandy and Jamison?"

She looked at him in the mirror. "Yeah, but I thought it was just because of the Luke Cage and Jessica Jones thing." Her eyes got big, then showed dismay, but then hope. She wasn't thrilled that two parts of her life she'd so carefully sectioned off might be mixing, but was also happy for her friends. "You think it's more?"

"Possibly. We should get back out there, but first," he pulled her to him, kissed her nose, "I'd like to point out that in one year, we've completely merged — our homes, our friends, our things, our bodies, our *lives*. You are my other half. My partner. My lover. My everything, *Bellula*. These are now *our* friends — not my friends and your friends."

Ronnie turned and let him hold her. She needed his arms around her before she said what she'd wanted to tell him for months, but hadn't been able to.

"You healed me. Or maybe you gave me a safe space to finally allow the healing to happen, but however you want to phrase it, I was still broken when I met you, and within a week, I wasn't broken anymore. You're my everything too, you know." She leaned into him, soaking in his strength. "I know you keep telling me not to worry about the difference in our lifespans, but I worry about you. I'm going to grow old and die, eventually. I *know* I live a lot longer than humans, but I won't live centuries, much less millennia."

"We have options, my impatient little tiger, but I can't speak of them with you for another eleven years. Please trust me. Have I let you down yet?"

She took a breath. "No, but you also never told me there were options before."

He gave her a roguish smile. "We've hit the one year mark, and I don't believe Abbott will enforce consequences for sharing such a teeny little piece of a secret. He likes you. He won't want you to be worried."

Ronnie smiled and let him lead her back upstairs, her final concern assuaged. She'd been worried that her *happily ever after* would one day be a heartbreak for him, but if there was a way around the fact she'd die and leave him alone, then everything was, indeed, right with her world.

Stay up to date on Candace's new releases by signing up for her newsletter: bit.ly/cb-new-release.

Keep reading for an excerpt from Hallowed Destiny!

Candace Blevins

Bibliography

If you enjoyed *Unhallowed Murder,* you may also like other books set in the same universe, though in different series.

Chattanooga Supernaturals series, paranormal romance:
- The Dragon King *(Aaron Drake's story, and the first time we meet Duke and Brain)*
- Riding the Storm *(Kendra and Eric's story)*
- Acceptable Risk *(Bethany, Ranger, Mac, and Jonathan's story)*
- Careful What You Ask For (*Britches story*)
- Hallowed Destiny – Forged by Darkness
- Uncaged (*Ghost's mother's story*)
- Cocky Queen
- Unhallowed Murder
- Unexpected Gifts

Only Human series, urban fantasy
- Only Human
- An Unhuman Journey
- Of Humans and Monsters
- Defining Human
- Edge of Humanity

Rolling Thunder Motorcycle Club Series
- Duke
- Brain
- Bash Volume I
- Bash Volume II
- Bash Volume III
- Horse
- Nix
- Gonzo (*where we first meet Britches/Briana*)
- Ghost
- Bud
- Razor
- Bubbles

The Dark Underbelly of The Chattanooga Supernaturals
- Pride (*A short story featuring The Lion King*)
- Indentured Freedom: Owned by the Vampire (*Gavin*)
- Leashed (*Abbott*)
- An Elegant Weapon (*Bran*)

A Dark(ish) Faerie Tale
- Slave
- Lady
- Consort
- Queen

The *Safeword* series, intense BDSM contemporary romance

- Safeword Rainbow
- Safeword: Davenport
- Safewords: Davenport and Chiffon
- Safeword: Quinacridone
- Safeword: Matte *(Sam and Ethan Levi's story, we first meet Frisco and Cassie)*
- Safeword: Matte – In Training
- No Safeword: Matte – The Honeymoon
- No Safeword: Matte – Happily Ever After
- Safeword: Arabesque *(Frisco, Cassie, Isaac, and Cam's story)*
- Safeword: Mayday (TBA)

Check out other books by Candace Blevins at candaceblevins.com.

Keep reading for an excerpt from *Hallowed Destiny*!

Hallowed Destiny

Forged by Darkness

It's been a year since Destiny was abducted by sick demon worshipers who intended to use her as a human sacrifice. They'd already carved evil-looking symbols all over her body when she somehow managed to escape.

Tonight is Halloween — the one-year anniversary of her abduction — and she's determined to return to the woods where she nearly lost her life. She doesn't expect to see a white lion waiting for her. Aren't black cats supposed to be bad luck on Halloween? Perhaps a white lion will be the opposite of evil. Or, maybe she's finally lost her mind, because lions are *not* indigenous to Tennessee and Georgia.

Chapter One

Destiny

I parked at a diner just outside the Chickamauga Battlefield and pulled my bicycle out of the back of my SUV. I made sure my phone was in one pocket, pepper spray in another, and felt my exercise bra to be sure my dad's two-hundred-dollar flashlight was still secure. I hadn't told him I was borrowing it because I didn't want to answer all the questions about why I needed it. As far as my family was concerned, I was spending the night with a friend and staying in where it was safe.

A year ago tonight — Halloween — I'd been abducted by sick demon worshipers, and would've been killed by them as a human sacrifice had I not found a way to escape. They carved symbols into the flesh of my chest, stomach, thighs, feet, and hands. I'd forever have to wear bangs to hide the scars on my forehead.

On my eighteenth birthday two weeks ago, I'd had the first part of an extensive tattoo started on my chest. I planned to cover the horrible, *evil* scars with something beautiful, but it'd take a while.

Dread pooled in my stomach as I pedaled toward the spot I'd been staked to the ground. They'd stripped me naked and spread me out so it was impossible to hide any part of myself from them. They'd apparently wanted a virgin to kill in offering to whatever sick deity they worship.

To keep it from happening again, I'd planned to have sex with the first person who came along afterwards, but it hadn't worked out. The asshole I'd been dating — the one who'd claimed to be a *good Christian boy* — broke up with me two days later because he was afraid the marks on my skin made me evil.

Much to my parents' chagrin, I'd turned my back on the church and started dating the star quarterback at the local high school — with every intention of giving myself to him at the first opportunity, though they weren't aware of that last part. He lived two doors down so it hadn't been difficult to sneak and see him when I told them I was going for a bike ride.

Unfortunately, I'd freaked and started crying when he got my panties off, and he'd told me I was too high maintenance.

So a year later I was still a damned virgin, and may end up staying that way. Those *fuckers* had messed me up in the head, and when the quarterback had undressed me, my only thoughts in were how I'd felt when my kidnappers had stripped me and staked me spread-eagled on the ground.

My pastor's wife told me I needed to find a way to put this behind me — to close the door on it and look forward. I wasn't sure how to do that but figured going back to the scene of the crime on Halloween night was a good start. I'd researched the area on Google Earth and found what I hoped was the best spot to ride my bike into the woods. I looked all around to be sure no cars were near, and flicked my bike's headlight off as I veered into the pitch dark of the forest.

I stopped a few yards in because I couldn't see *anything*, and I planted my feet on either side of my bike and waited for my eyes to adjust to the dark. My heart raced and my pulse thundered in my ears, but I assured myself no one else could hear it.

Several long minutes later, I thought I might be able to pick out the trees, but not well enough to walk, much less ride. I propped my bike on a tree with a sigh, and turned the flashlight to the lowest setting. I hadn't planned to use it this close to the road, but it didn't look like I had a choice.

Each step forward took every bit of willpower I possessed. I wanted to turn and run back to the road, but I just *knew* I'd never move past this unless I could face my fears. If I could walk into the woods on Halloween and stand in the spot I'd fought my abductors, perhaps I'd be brave enough to have sex with someone and finally lose my pesky virginity.

I counted fifty steps before I turned the flashlight a little brighter, and I pulled my phone from my pocket and re-engaged the directions to the GPS coordinates I'd chosen. I hoped the location I'd found on the map would get me close enough so I'd be able to find *the spot* once I was nearby.

I had crazy dreams about that night. It often felt more like I'd been rescued, but I also kind of vaguely remembered getting an arm free and grabbing the knife from one of the men, and then going to town on my kidnappers as I cut myself free. But then there was the dream where a woman levitated me up to sit on a tree branch while monsters fought monsters. Were there good monsters? Some of them looked half-human and half-animal, truly grotesque… and yet in my dreams they fought the evil men who'd abducted me.

I had less than a quarter mile to walk, but it felt like I crept miles in the dark — carefully placing each foot and listening for sounds of anything larger than a possum while my own pulse thundered in my ears.

When I finally arrived at the GPS spot, I turned my dad's flashlight to full strength — all twenty-eight hundred lumens.

And was shocked to see a white lion sitting fifty yards away.

I couldn't move. Couldn't breathe. My feet were cemented to the ground as the lion looked down and away as the too-bright light must've hurt his eyes.

Two seconds later he turned and gracefully leapt through the air, and within seconds he'd run off to the side and out of the beam. I turned the light in every direction but couldn't find him again. Had I hallucinated him? Lions are *not* indigenous to Tennessee. Or Georgia. Crap, I was just over the line in Georgia. Didn't matter. There shouldn't be a lion.

Hallowed Destiny is available at major retail outlets.

About the Author:

Candace Blevins has published more than forty books. She lives with her husband of twenty years and their two daughters. When not working or driving young teens all over the place, she can be found reading, writing, meditating, or swimming. The family's beloved, goofy, retired racing greyhound is usually at her side as she writes, quietly keeping her company.

Candace writes Urban Fantasy, Paranormal Romance, Contemporary BDSM Romance, and a kick-ass Motorcycle Club series.

Her urban fantasy series, *Only Human*, gives us a world where weredragons, werewolves, werelions, three different species of vampires, and a variety of other mythological beings exist.

Candace's two paranormal romance series, *The Chattanooga Supernaturals* and *The Rolling Thunder Motorcycle Club*, are both sister series to the *Only Human* series, and give some secondary characters their happily ever after.

Her *Dark(ish) Faerie Tale* series gives us a close-up and personal look at Queen Mab, and her *Dark Underbelly* series is, as you'd expect, dark and (if you're a little twisted) oh-so-yummy.

Her contemporary *Safeword* series gives us characters who happen to have some extreme kinks. Relationships can be difficult enough without throwing power exchange into the mix, and her books show characters who care enough about each other to fight to make the relationship work. Each couple in the Safeword series gives the reader a different take on the lifestyle.

You can visit Candace on the web at candaceblevins.com and feel free to friend her on Facebook at facebook.com/candacesblevins and Goodreads at goodreads.com/CandaceBlevins. You can also join facebook.com/groups/CandacesKinksters to get sneak peeks into what she's writing now, images that inspire her, and the occasional juicy teaser.

Stay up to date on Candace's newest releases, and get exclusive excerpts by joining her mailing list at bit.ly/cb-new-release !

Made in United States
Orlando, FL
09 October 2022

23186759R00133